ALSO BY MARYANN McFADDEN

The Richest Season

Cape Cod Light
(Formerly titled *So Happy Together*)

The Book Lover

The Cemetery Keeper's Wife

THE
CHRISTMAS STAR

the Christmas Star

A
Holiday
Romance

MARY·ANN McFADDEN

For my mother, who told me I needed to write about the star

*For my grands: Alice, Lily-Sam, Julia, Phoebe & Jackson, who teach
me every day that family is everything*

*And for all those who have kept the star shining
and continue to do so*

CHAPTER 1

HOPE REYNOLDS OPENED THE FRONT door of her house, a warm Carolina breeze lifting her shoulder-length brown hair. Though it was already December, it was so mild she could have been wearing shorts or a sundress. Instead, she had on jeans and a cardigan, knowing how quickly the weather would change on this journey north.

Wheeling her suitcase down the brick walk, she stopped suddenly, her stomach squeezing so hard she could barely take a breath. The "For Sale" sign on her front lawn was now plastered with giant red letters: "UNDER CONTRACT." Her landlord, she thought, was the embodiment of Ebeneezer Scrooge. Not only wouldn't he give her the four weeks she'd begged for to see if she could buy the house. Now, just weeks before Christmas, he'd obviously gotten a buyer and didn't even have the good grace to tell her. Nor did her friend Lily next door, who was his realtor. This was so not fair. She'd been a perfect tenant for the past three years.

Behind her, the front door opened and her nine-year-old son, Zach, stumbled out sleepily in a t-shirt and shorts, carrying a backpack. She quickly moved to block the sign.

"Zach, Honey, you need to wear the clothes I put on your bed. It's going to get cold as we head north," she called out to him.

Zach stopped and pouted. "Can't I just stay here with Lily, Mom? Jackson's coming over later with his new skateboard. He says it's awesome."

She looked at her son, his dirty blonde hair stuck up in bedhead spikes, his Pokemon t-shirt with a juice stain from yesterday obviously yanked from his hamper. Still so much a little boy. Yet sometimes a hint of the young man he would one day become making little appearances when they'd talk about something serious. As they did last night about this trip.

Hope walked over to him, took his backpack, and hung it on her suitcase handle.

"Do you really want to miss seeing your first snow?" she asked with a teasing smile.

Zach looked up at her with a begrudging tilt to his lips. "Can we go sleigh riding?"

Last night she'd told him there probably wouldn't be much time for that. Now she looked at those serious green eyes, so much like his father's. "Of course."

His face lit up and she was rewarded with a hug. "Okaaaaay!" And then he pulled away. "But Mom, we're gonna be home for Christmas, right? For Dad to get me?"

"Honey, Christmas is three weeks away. We'll be back in plenty of time. Now go change into those clothes on your bed. And please toss those back in the hamper."

She watched him go back inside, shaking her head. Then

she wheeled the suitcase and backpack to her SUV in the drive-way and opened the trunk. Last night she'd put in coats and other things to make this morning easier to get on the road.

"So you're really going home?"

Hope turned to find Lily Abbott, her neighbor and pseu-do-aunt to Zach, walking over, already dressed for her day in heels, with her blonde pageboy picture perfect.

"This is home, Lil. At least until you close on it." She tried so hard to keep the sound of disappointment out of her voice.

"Listen, Sweetie, I'm so sorry I wasn't able to fill you in before my sign guy posted the Under Contract. He wasn't supposed to do that."

She stood there, biting her lip, forcing back the tears. Lily had been so good to her and Zach, taking them under her wing from the moment they moved in three years ago. How could she be mad at her? A decade older than Hope, she was like the big sister Hope had always longed for.

"I'm sorry, I know it's not your fault. I just wish he would have given me until the end of the month so I'd know if I'm keeping my job or not. He knew I was hoping to buy it. I don't want to move Zach again, Lil. He's been through enough and he just loves it here."

"Listen, you will keep your job. The *Tribune* would be crazy to let you go. Your articles are always the best thing in there."

"We'll see. We have three feature writers and now with ad space diminishing they're cutting us down to one. So, two of us writers will be getting the axe before the new year."

"I didn't realize it was that bad."

"I've got one more special assignment to deliver for

Christmas and that'll decide my fate."

"I'm sure you'll wow them. Your Thanksgiving piece about the homeless group living on the beach had me in tears it was so beautiful."

"I hope you're right."

"And then I promise, I'll find you a great house to buy, and not too far from ME!"

"Thanks, I know you'll do your best."

"So ... how long has it been? Since you've gone ... back."

Hope sighed, shaking her head. "Actually, since my mom passed away. A long time. But I need to do this. There are all of her things in the attic, and some of mine, too. I don't want it getting tossed when my dad moves to Florida."

"Wow. So ... you haven't seen your dad since?"

"Once, when Zach was two. It didn't go well, unfortunately. He never really cared for Drew."

"Sounds like this'll be a tough trip. Sure you don't want help?"

Hope shook her head. "I need to get this done quickly then come straight back and get my article written. And Drew is supposed to take Zach for Christmas. He's pretty excited. His dad is taking him to Hawaii."

"Wow, that's pretty extravagant," Lily said with raised eyebrows.

"I know. Which makes me wonder."

"Another new girlfriend?"

"Wouldn't surprise me. I wish he wouldn't put Zach through that."

"Think your ex will really show?"

She sighed, shaking her head. "He'd better show. Zach is so excited about going to Hawaii. Drew promised to teach him to surf, though that in itself makes me nervous."

Just then the front door opened and Zach came out in jeans and a long sleeve t-shirt, shuffling down the walk.

"Come here, you," Lily said, pulling him into a hug.

"Tell Jackson I'm going sleigh riding!" he said with a fist pump.

"Sleigh riding! Oh, I'm sure he's going to be jealous."

Hope opened the back door and Zach climbed in.

"When you get back, Honey, I'm taking you and Jackson to the new arcade down at the beach. My Christmas present," Lily said. "Now you have a great trip!"

"I'll make sure he does. No matter how much I don't want to go back," Hope said, after closing his door.

She gave Lily a quick hug, got in, and checked to make sure Zach was buckled up. He was already zoned out on a video game. Looking into the rear-view mirror to back out, she wound up looking right at herself. Staring back at her were gray eyes that told of little sleep lately, worry lines already forming around the edges. It wasn't just the possible loss of her job and the move. It was the stress of this trip and all of the emotions it was dredging up. And the one person she wished she could call, who could somehow talk her through this and make her believe it would all be okay, that person was long gone.

Ninety minutes later they were on Route 95, heading north.

It was a twelve-hour drive without complications, and she hoped they'd get there without Zach getting car sick. They'd already stopped once on the winding South Carolina backroads and luckily his stomach settled right down. She warned Zach to put away the video games and just look out the window.

"But it's boring!" he'd complained.

She'd prayed he'd fall asleep. It was going to be a long drive back to New Jersey.

He'd been quiet for a while now and she was thankful for the book downloads she'd gotten, his favorite *Dogman* series, as well as the *Diary of a Wimpy Kid* sequel. As the mile markers flew by and the hours ticked away, her mind kept traveling back to the last time she saw her father. *Don't go there*, she cautioned herself each time. Because inevitably it would end in the usual inner war of guilt and anger, and neither one was something she wanted to dwell on right now.

Instead, she let her thoughts drift to memories of her mother, despite an ache of grief in her chest that felt like it was squeezing her heart. It was Christmas and she was going back to Hackettstown. How could she not think of her mother? But how was it possible she'd been gone so long? Ten years. Her mother had not been there to see her get married. When she was pregnant with Zach she cried so often, wishing she had her mother to turn to during those middle-of-the-night moments of anxiety. What if something went wrong? Would her baby be healthy? Would she be a good mother? But even more emotional was wanting to share those pure moments of joy after her baby was born. When she held Zach for the first time, that tiny face staring up at her with a little frown, as if to say *who are you and how did I get here,* she'd burst into tears, picturing her mother holding her when she was born and feeling the same joy inside of her. A love unlike anything she'd ever felt before. And a fierce protective determination, like a lioness for her cub. Hope vowed she would spend her life making sure nothing ever hurt this innocent child.

"Mom," Zach said, suddenly interrupting her thoughts. "I'm hungry."

She smiled, glancing in the rearview mirror, tilted so she could keep an eye on him.

"Okay, Honey, we're on straight roads now, so you can open the cooler next to you. There's a bagel with cream cheese and some fruit and chocolate milk."

"Is it—"

"Yes, it's a cinnamon raisin bagel, your favorite."

"Thanks, Mom."

"But stay off the video games for a while. We don't want another side-of-the-road emergency stop," she said with a little laugh.

"I know," Zach said with an agreeable little grumble.

Only ten hours and two more meals to go.

It was dark when they hit the New Jersey backroads, a quicker route to Hackettstown, which was in the northwest corner of the state. When Hope told people where she was from, they usually pictured Newark Airport or Atlantic City. Hope had to tell them that the small town was in farming country and that it was more like Vermont than New York City. That it was a beautiful little valley surrounded by small mountains that encircled it like loving arms. She wasn't sure anyone really believed her.

Zach fell asleep again after a while and Hope listened to an old audiobook on writing, *Thunder and Lightning,* by Natalie Goldberg. She should have started her article for the *Tribune* a week ago, but she just couldn't focus what with her house going on the market and this trip coming up. Now the audiobook spoke to her creative core, inspiring her, and ideas for her Christmas article began to flow. When they stopped for the night, she would jot some of them down quickly before bed so she wouldn't forget.

When she finally drove past Budd Lake, all frozen over and dotted with little campfires as people ice-fished, she turned the book off, glancing at Zach in the backseat, headphones around his neck, eyes closed.

"Zach, we're almost to Hackettstown. Look out your window."

She smiled, glancing back again, as Zach rubbed his eyes and turned to look out the window. His eyes grew wide and his mouth fell open.

"Mom, it's snowing!"

Hope smiled, her heart swelling at his sudden joy. "Yes, it is!"

"Wow, everything is white!"

"It sure is, Honey."

"It's so cool!

"Zach, do you remember me telling you about the

Christmas Star I used to wish on when I was a little girl? Pretty soon you're going to see it. It's really special."

"Does it really look like the star is hanging up in the sky over the whole town?"

"It sure does."

"And did your wishes always come true?"

"Well … sometimes my wishes came true but not in the way I thought they would. But that was okay."

"Can I make a wish on it?"

"Of course, you can."

"I can't tell you, though, Mom."

"I know, that's okay. Now get ready. See how there are woods outside? That means we're almost to Hackettstown Mountain."

"Is it a really big mountain?"

"Big enough."

"Cool."

The highway split in two and a moment later, they were starting to descend the mountain. Snow-covered trees lined the side of the mountain road, but Hope kept glancing to her right across the windshield waiting for the woods to break.

"Keep looking out your window, Zach," she urged him, and a few moments later, suddenly, there it was. "Look! See the lights of the town below?"

"Is that Hackettstown?"

"Yes, that's Hackettstown," she exclaimed, a catch of emotion in her voice. At that moment it truly hit her how long it had been. The lights of the small town spread out across the valley.

"It looks like our Christmas village. It's really pretty, but

… I don't see the star."

She was watching the road again, realizing she'd been swerving a bit. "It's on top of Buck Hill. Look across the valley, there … "

"I don't see it, Mom."

Hope put her blinker on and pulled over to the shoulder. Stretching to look out the right-side passenger window, she looked across the lights of the valley, the town all lit up like a Norman Rockwell night scene. There was the gold dome of the college, the tall white spire of the Presbyterian church, and the gas lanterns lining Main Street, but above it all, on top of Buck Hill across the valley … there was no star.

"It's … gone." She sat there, numb, unable to believe this was possible.

"What happened? You said it's always there, every December."

"I know, Honey, I'm not sure. It must be a power outage or something." She could hear the tremble in her voice.

"You okay, Mom?"

Hope nodded, turning to smile and reassure Zach. "Of course. Listen, we'll be at the B&B in just a few minutes and we can find out tomorrow what's going on. I'm sure whatever it is will be fixed quickly."

"Okay, Mom. We'll see."

She pulled back on the road, lamenting Zach's "we'll see." Oh, he'd caught onto that game apparently, how "we'll see" was usually a delay tactic for something that wasn't actually going to happen.

She continued down the mountain as pressure built in her ears. "Zach, swallow a couple of times so your ears pop."

After a moment, Zach laughed. "Wow, Mom, that is so cool. My ears did pop. What happened?"

"Oh, it's just pressure from the elevation going down. That's how I always knew I was almost home."

At the bottom of the mountain, the road widened to both lanes again. A few minutes later, they crossed over the Musconetcong River and slowed down as they approached Main Street, which looked like something out of a Christmas card. Gas lanterns lined the sidewalks on both sides, adorned with big green wreaths festooned with holly and glittering red bows. The shops and cafés on either side were all decked out with lights and garlands, though most were already closed.

"Mom," Zach called excitedly, "can we go to that cool candy store tomorrow?"

She looked out her window to see a sign for Phoebe's Candy Shoppe, with M&M figures standing guard out front beside several life-size gingerbread men.

"Sure thing, Zach, once we get settled. Don't forget, I've got some serious work to get done here and we don't have a lot of time."

"I know. And I've got my schoolwork."

"Yes, you do."

At the corner of Main and Grand, Hope took a right and headed up a block to the Emerson House Bed & Breakfast. As she pulled into the parking lot, her heart sank.

"Mom, there's no lights on in there."

No, it couldn't be. She meant to call ahead for a reservation but in the flurry of getting ready had forgotten. She didn't think it mattered, really, because the Emerson House had been there for as long as she could remember and there were always vacancies, especially on a weeknight. She pulled out her cell phone and googled the number, which took her to the website, which announced they were … retired.

"Mom?"

She could hear the worry in Zach's voice.

"It's fine, Zach, just a little change of plans. Maybe this is for the best, anyway. I just didn't want to arrive too late to your grandfather's, so I thought we'd stay here tonight. Anyway, it's only a little after ten. We should be fine."

"That's not so late."

She smiled. "No, it's not."

Besides, maybe it was better to rip the band-aid off all at once. She started the car up again.

Hope pulled out of the B&B and went back to Main Street, turning west to the far side of town.

"Is that the mountain over there, Buck Hill?" Zach asked.

"Yes, that's it," she said, looking up at it through the windshield. "The house I grew up in is just a few blocks away."

A few blocks later she turned onto Linwood Street and her eyes suddenly filled with tears. Oh … she had to keep it together. For Zach. But she was suddenly so flooded with memories. It was one of the most charming streets in town, with a median that ran up the middle, separating the street. In the spring, flowering cherries bloomed as far up as you could see and one of her favorite times was when the wind would blow the blossoms into the air and it seemed as though it was snowing pink petals all around her. Now, though, that strip of land was dark, but the houses that lined the block were all lit up for Christmas. Two blocks up, she pulled into the driveway of a white Cape Cod draped in icicle lights from all of the eaves. Candles were lit in all the windows and garlands draped the front porch, twinkling with colored lights. Lights were on inside, too, thank goodness. Her dad was still up.

"Okay, Zach."

"Wow, Mom, it's a really pretty house."

It looked exactly the way her mother had always had it decorated. She swallowed hard, fighting the lump of emotion threatening to undo her. "Yes, it really is."

She got out and opened his door, took his hand and they walked up the small porch. Hope knocked on the door and it felt surreal, standing there, waiting for someone to answer. She had never done that before. But she didn't feel comfortable just walking in. After all, this hadn't been her home in more than a decade. It might feel strange, like walking into a stranger's house, but one that was somehow filled with her memories. Her legs, she realized, were trembling, and not just from twelve hours on the gas pedal.

The door opened and Hope's eyes widened in surprise. Julia Timbrook, her mother's best friend, and their next-door neighbor for decades, stood there, her hair in a short gray bob now, wearing a Christmas apron. Julia broke into a big smile.

"Hope!"

"Julia ... " she stammered, "do you live here now?"

"Oh, no, no, I still live next door, Hope. I was just helping your dad get ready. He thought you'd be here in the morning.

"Yes, we were supposed to … I thought we'd stay at the B&B since it's so late, but I guess they've closed."

"Oh, they've been closed a few years now. But I'm so happy to see you! Your dad will be, too. He's thrilled you've finally come home."

"Julia, we'll be heading back south in a few days, *that's* home."

Julia's smile faded. "Oh … of course. Well, come inside, both of you. We can get your things in a bit."

"I'm sorry, that came out harsh," she said, as Julia closed the door. "It's just that I have a lot to do while I'm here. Zach's got Christmas plans and I've got an article I need to finish."

"An article?" Julia interrupted. "You're still writing! Your mother would be so happy. I am, too. And I was so sorry to hear about your—"

Now Hope interrupted her. "I'm just here to go through my mother's things and then we'll be on our way, Julia."

Julia nodded quietly, then turned with a smile

"And you must be Zach."

"Zach, Honey, this is Julia. Mrs. Timbrook. She lives next door."

Julia bent down and ruffled Zach's hair. "I was your grandma's best friend, Zach. And I think I see a little bit of her in those beautiful dimples of yours. Your grandfather is so happy you've come."

"Where is my dad, by the way?" Hope asked.

"He's out back getting some wood."

Just then they heard the back door slam. "Julia?" she heard her father's voice call.

"We're in the hall, Red," Julia called back. "You'll never guess who's here."

A moment later Red McClain came slowly into the foyer in jeans and a flannel shirt. His red hair was now completely gray and he looked so much thinner than when she last saw him. Her father looked at her for a long moment, his face full of emotion. And then he turned to Zach and she could see him struggling to find his voice.

"Are you my grandfather," Zach asked shyly.

For a moment her father didn't speak, then he cleared his throat. "Why yes, I am. And you must be Zach."

Zach held his little hand out and her father shook it.

"Nice to meet you, young man. You've got a good, strong grip."

"Thanks, so do you. My dad says you can tell a lot about a person by how they shake hands."

"I'd say that's very true." And then her dad looked at her again. "Hello, Hope. How are you?"

She fought the lump in her throat so hard. For a moment she couldn't speak, either, and just nodded her head with a smile that seemed to take everything from her. Then she pulled Zach to her, her arm around his shoulders.

"We're great, Dad. But exhausted after all that driving, right Zach?"

Zach nodded.

"Well, I bet you've got a little more energy left for some Christmas cookies and hot cocoa?" Julia cajoled.

Zach's face lit up. "Can I, Mom?"

How could she say no to that face? And after he'd been

so good on that grueling drive. She nodded and Julia led Zach into the kitchen. Then Hope was there alone with her father.

"I'm so glad you're home, Sweetheart. I hope you'll stay for Christmas. It's been so long, and Zach—"

And now came the words she rehearsed during the long drive. "Dad, I'm really sorry, but I've only got a few days. Zach has school and Drew is taking him for Christmas, so … " It was hard to continue with the disappointment on her father's face.

"Aren't you ever going to forgive me?"

"There's nothing to forgive."

Her father shook his head, looking away for a moment. And then his eyes landed on the picture frames on the hall table. He was looking at her mother.

"Dad, please, can we just let it go?"

He looked at her and nodded in resignation.

"Dad, what happened to the star?"

"The star was partially destroyed in a big Nor'easter a few years back. Half the town was damaged."

"I can't believe it. That star's been shining over this town every Christmas for more than 75 years."

"I know. People tried to raise money and all, but there was so much else to be fixed."

Now Hope looked at the photos. "Mom would be heartbroken."

"I know that. She used to wish on that star as a little girl from her bedroom upstairs. And then you did the same. That star is part of our family history."

"Well, nothing's forever. I think we both know that now."

Hope pulled her keys out of her pocket and turned to the door, to get the rest of their things. "Anyway, I've got to get Zach to bed, it's been a long day."

"Hope."

She turned.

"At least let me show Zach a real Hackettstown Christmas for whatever time you're here, okay?"

"Sure," she said, before going outside.

Neither of them noticed Zach peeking in at them, listening. Before his grandfather turned, he quickly went back into the kitchen.

It was nearly eleven and Zach was still awake in one twin bed in his mom's old bedroom, while she unpacked their suitcases on the other twin bed. The house was really pretty inside, but it was old and made noises and he asked her if they could share the room tonight.

Now he watched his mom close the suitcase and put it on a chair, then walk to the window and look out. He knew what she was thinking, and how disappointed she was. She'd told him so many times how she could see the star from her pillow, where he was lying right now. She was always so excited when she told him. And he wanted to lay here and see it and make his own wishes. He had lots of them.

Hope turned from the window and took her stack of folded clothes and put them in the empty dresser drawers. She'd always loved her bedroom, with its dormers and peaks, even though as she grew, she'd sometimes hit her head in the corners. She even told Lily once, before her rental had come up for sale, that she'd love to find a Cape Cod just like this house. As her gaze took in every detail, it seemed as if time had stood still in this room and she was still a young girl, with everything in life ahead of her. Every dream still a hope, and a promise.

Who could have possibly predicted how it would have all turned out? That her mother would leave them so young, that she herself would stay away for years. And that one day she'd return at thirty-four years old, a divorced single mother. But now, everywhere she turned in this house, in this room, there was a memory coming to life in her head. Her mother bustling in the kitchen, always singing as she cooked. Her dad, younger, still with red hair, giving her a piggyback ride up the stairs to bed. And she herself sitting at her little desk in the corner there, writing in her journal she'd gotten for her tenth birthday, the pink one with its precious lock and key.

But mostly, she could see herself at just about Zach's age, standing at the window, so excited the first night the star was lit, her mother standing beside her.

I'm so excited to see the star again, Mommy. It's been a whole year and I have lots of wishes!

She could hear her mother's voice as if it were a whisper in the darkness now, as if she were really there: *Well, all my wishes have come true, Sweetheart. I've got you.*

She watched as if it were really happening, her mother taking her hand, leading her to bed, then tucking her in. And then that little girl version of herself turned from her pillow to look out the window again. To see the star from her bed, her special place. Her mother was sitting beside her, stroking her hair, then kissing her good night. She'd lay there until she couldn't keep her eyes open any longer, making her wishes.

If a heart could truly break from grief, she thought as she went back to the window and looked up at the darkness, the vision disappearing, hers would be crumbling right now. Her chest ached with sadness and longing.

"I miss you so much, Mom," she whispered. "And I miss our star. It always gave me hope."

CHAPTER 2

ZACH WOKE BEFORE HIS MOM. He slipped out of bed and carried his clothes to the bathroom across the hall. He figured it was before seven, the time he usually got up for school, because it was just getting light out. After he dressed, he tiptoed down the stairs and quietly went out the front door, walking quickly down the street until he came to a dirt road and saw the sign: *Buck Hill, Private Lane.* It had snowed some more during the night and his sneakers were already wet, but he began trudging up the lane. He had to do this for his mom.

The road was steep and he was breathing hard, but the woods were so white and pretty. And everything was so quiet. He should've been cold, but he was starting to sweat. He kept looking up ahead, hoping to see the star, but there were just tall trees. Finally, he reached the top, a big open clearing, and there it was, a giant structure that didn't really look like it could be a star. It was bad. He remembered learning how to draw a star in art, the five points of it. The top point and the two side points of the star were bent and twisted and pieces of the metal were missing. It was still really high, almost to the tops of the trees. It was just the bottom two points that made it look like it could've been a star. He walked closer, touching it, looking up and wondering if—

"Hey, what do you think you're doing?"

He turned, scared suddenly, and a big black and white dog came running toward him, barking.

"Kodi, sit!"

The dog stopped suddenly and Zach saw the man coming now. He hadn't noticed the house or the jeep on the other side of the clearing. The man limped a little. Zach was terrified, he knew he was in trouble.

"This is private property. What are you doing here?" the man asked.

Zach couldn't let his fear take over. "I was trying to find out what's wrong with the star. I need it to work for my mom. She's sad and maybe it'll make her happy again."

"I'm sorry your mom is sad. It can't be fixed though." The man stopped beside the dog and began petting it. "Does your mom know you're here?"

Zach looked guiltily at the ground and shook his head. The man looked a little older than his mom. His voice was kinder now and he didn't seem mean.

"How about I take you home before she sends out a search party."

"Could you please not tell her I came all the way up here alone? She worries a lot."

"Sure. What's your name?"

"Zach Reynolds. I'm nine."

"Nice to meet you, Zach. I'm Ryan and this here is Kodi.

Let me just close up my workshop."

Zach followed Ryan and Kodi across the driveway to a wood building beside a house. When they went inside, it was full of wood and tools and a big workbench and saw. There were pieces of assorted Christmas decorations all over the place. Kodi came and sat by Zach.

"Do you make things?" Zach asked.

"I do," Ryan said, stopping by the workbench and gathering tools. "I work with wood and make all sorts of things like furniture and birdhouses. Whatever people are willing to pay for."

Zach walked over to a life-size reindeer leaning against the wall, a few antlers missing. "And Christmas decorations?"

"I'm just repairing those. They're very old and the town is going to use them again because the newer ones got destroyed in the same storm that damaged the star."

Zach looked at him. "If you fix things, maybe you can fix the star?"

"I'm afraid not," Ryan said, shaking his head. "It's beyond repair."

"But ... "

But Ryan was getting his keys and walking to the door. As Zach walked over, his eyes landed on something and he stopped. "Is this a sled?"

"An old one, but yes, it is. Haven't you ever seen a sled before?"

Zach shook his head. "I live in South Carolina. It doesn't snow there."

Ryan nodded, then turned to his dog. "Kodi, stay. I'll be

right back."

Zach followed Ryan to his black pick-up truck, hoping he wasn't in big trouble.

Hope was surprised she slept until nearly eight o'clock. And that Zach's bed was empty. The smell of coffee greeted her as she went downstairs. Her father was sitting at the breakfast bar, reading the paper.

"Where's Zach?" she asked, looking around.

Her father put the paper down. "Isn't he still sleeping?"

"No. He's probably outside in the snow. He's so excited by it." She looked out the back door.

Her dad got up and looked out the window. "I don't think so, Honey. I've been up a while."

"But where on earth could he be?" She hurried into the foyer and saw his jacket gone from the coat tree. A drumbeat of nerves began in her stomach. "Dad, his coat is gone!"

Just then there was a loud knock on the front door. Hope threw it open. There was Zach, face flushed with cold, standing beside a man.

"Zach, oh my gosh, where have you been? I was worried sick."

"I ... went to find the star."

Hope looked up at the man beside her son, dressed for some kind of construction job, who must've found him on his way to work. "Thank you so much for bringing him home."

"I'm Ryan Miller," he said, reaching out to shake her hand.

"Hope McL ... I mean Reynolds. How did you find him?"

"I live on top of Buck Hill."

"Next to the star?"

He had clear blue eyes and for a moment she saw a flicker of something there. "Yes," he said, then he looked at her father. "Hi Red. I brought my tools, figure if it's okay I'll get an early start on those beams." He picked up a toolbox she hadn't noticed.

She looked from the man to her father. "Wait … you two know each other?"

Her father smiled. "Ryan's a heck of a handyman. He's helping me get the house ready to put on the market after Christmas."

"Mom," Zach said, pulling her hand, forcing her to look at him. "Ryan says the star can't be fixed."

She looked at Ryan. "If you live in the house then you own the star and all the land on top of Buck Hill."

"That's right."

"And … you're apparently a heck of a handyman. But … you just gave up on the star."

Ryan's face turned pink. "Christmas … well, it isn't really my thing."

"Hope, Honey," her dad interrupted, "it's bad."

She looked from one to the other until Ryan finally said, "I should get to work now." He turned and gave Zach a wink. She watched him go upstairs, noticing a slight limp. Then she turned to Zach and put both hands on his shoulders.

"Young man, don't you ever give me a scare like that again, do you hear?"

"I'm sorry, Mom. I promise."

She pulled him into a fierce hug until Zach began to squirm and she let him go.

"Okay, then, let's get some breakfast, then I need to get started on the attic. And you can do some schoolwork."

"Can we go to that candy store first? The one we passed last night? You promised, Mom."

She looked at her son, those pleading green eyes, the flushed face. He was really such a good kid and this little scare wasn't like him. "Okay, just a quick trip. And then schoolwork."

"You're the best, Mom," Zach said, running into the kitchen.

Somehow, at that moment, she felt anything but. She wondered what Drew would say if he knew Zach had been missing like that.

Later that morning, after Hope and Zach left for town, Red McClain sat in his kitchen staring out the back window. Not really looking at anything. He thought he'd prepared himself for this visit with his daughter and his grandson, but he'd been sorely mistaken.

It was seven years since he'd last seen his daughter. Zach was just two, a chubby and rambunctious toddler who'd immediately stolen his heart. They'd just moved to Boston from New York because Drew had started a new position, climbing up the ladder of his family's business. Hope had put on a good front, but he could see there were cracks in the marriage already. Drew was rarely home and when he was, he seemed to have little patience for the noise and demands of a toddler.

Or the toys inevitably strewn about as Zach played. When Red asked Hope about her writing at dinner one night, Drew rolled his eyes.

How had he let seven years go by? It was his own fault, of course. If Alice hadn't left them, everything would have been different. She would have known what to do. Years wouldn't have been wasted like this. He'd bungled it all and had only himself to blame. But he didn't really have a choice, did he?

What made it all even harder was walking into the foyer last night and feeling his heart stop. It was as if his Alice was right there, young again, and so beautiful with those wide gray eyes and glossy brown hair. Hope looked so much like her. But where Alice's eyes were always lit with joy, his daughter's eyes were guarded. Closed off. And his initial hope began to sink.

But what nearly undid him was his grandson, now nine years old, no longer the chubby rambunctious toddler but a little boy with a firm handshake and the serious and inquisitive eyes of an old soul. If he'd had any doubt of that, it was proven that morning when Ryan brought Zach home. What courage it must have taken that little boy to find his way to the top of Buck Hill. Because he'd known how important the star was to his mother. Red's heart had almost burst with love.

He sat there in the kitchen, thinking about everything that had happened after Alice died. Berating himself for all of the time lost. What he knew now with certainty, despite his pride and guilt and little waves of anger, was that he'd wasted more time than he ever should have. And that the time was now to somehow make things right with Hope.

The only problem was, if he did, wouldn't it be a betrayal?

✳

Walking into town with her son, Hope realized that she and Zach never did this at home. The city center was too far, and there was no real downtown. Just highways and strip malls outside of their suburban neighborhood. Now, as they turned onto Main Street, everything looked so beautiful, the lanterns lit even in daylight, tiny white lights glowing in the storefronts, and big flakes of snow falling gently. Zach kept opening his mouth to catch them.

"Mom, this looks like our snow globe, doesn't it?"

He was actually skipping, something she couldn't remember him doing in at least a few years, being too big for such childish behavior.

"It sure does."

Everything looked the same, but still … there was something different. And of course, that was the way. She hadn't walked this street in over a decade. The town had changed. And so had she.

Then she thought about what lay ahead later that morning. When was the last time she'd been up in the attic, which was brimming with the artifacts of her family's lives? All of them with a story. A souvenir from a moment in time. Suddenly, the reality of what she was about to face, memories of her mother and her own girlhood she would soon be unearthing, seemed too overwhelming. Especially now.

"Mom! You're not listening."

"Oh, I'm sorry, Zach. I guess I'm a little distracted."

"Can we make a snowman later?"

"Sure."

Zach stopped then, taking her arm and forcing her to stop. "Are you sad, Mom? About the star?"

She looked at his worried little face. "Maybe a little. But you know what? Hackettstown has so much cool Christmas stuff maybe we won't miss it."

"Like what?"

"Pretty soon all these stores on Main Street will be making ice sculptures right here on the sidewalk for a contest in the Hometown Holiday. They'll take giant blocks of ice and use chainsaws and knives and make incredible Christmas figures."

"What's the Hometown Holiday?"

"Oh, it's like a big party in town that lasts for two whole weeks up until Christmas Eve. It starts with a Santa Parade and then there's a grand illumination by the college and a tree lighting at the town gazebo. There are horse and carriage rides and on the last night there's the Jingle Ball and everyone dances under a big white tent. It's magical."

"Even without the star?"

Hope crouched down so she was face-to-face with her son. "Zach, sometimes things in life change and there's not much we can do about it."

She watched her son's mind process this. "You mean like Dad leaving?"

She wanted to cry. Though it had been years since Drew left, she knew the hole it left in her son's heart. Drew hadn't just left her. He'd left this little boy.

"Yes, Honey, like Dad leaving. And if I could, I would make sure nothing ever happened to disappoint you. But …

we're doing okay, aren't we?"

Zach nodded, then broke into a smile. "And I get to go to Hawaii. Dad's gonna teach me how to surf."

"You're going to have an awesome time," she said, pulling him into a quick hug.

"HOPE! HOPE MCCLAIN! Is that you?"

Hope and Zach both turned to see a young woman in an apron with red curls bouncing as she ran toward them.

"Phoebe Hodge! I didn't realize ... is that your candy shop?"

Phoebe stopped and looked from Zach to her and back to Zach again. "It is you! I can't believe it! And yes, the store is my dream come true!"

Phoebe pulled Hope into a long hug and then reached out to shake Zach's hand.

"This is my son, Zach. And it's Hope Reynolds now."

"Do you get to eat all the candy you want?" Zach asked.

"I sure do," Phoebe said, with her classic lopsided grin. "My favorites are red Twizzlers. Why don't you come in and pick out some of yours?"

Phoebe led them past a few other shops to her store, where the life-size M&M figures were waving hello beside a bench on the sidewalk. Two giant gingerbread men stood on either side of her shop's door. Inside it was the kind of old-fashioned candy shop Hope remembered as a kid. Glass counters filled with chocolates, taffy, and fudge. On top were jars filled with colorful rock candy and gumballs. The opposite wall was lined with baskets of anything imaginable.

"Here you go, Zach," Phoebe said, handing him a red

basket. "Why don't you pick up some of your own favorites."

"Wow, really? Can I, Mom?"

"Sure, just don't go overboard."

As Zach wandered off, Phoebe turned back to Hope with an excited smile. "So, are you back for good?"

"Oh, no, not at all. My Dad's going to be selling the house and there's ... well, a lot of my mom's stuff still in the attic I need to sort through."

"That's got to be so hard for him. Your mom was the best. I swear the Hometown Holiday hasn't been the same without her. She just made it all happen like magic. Now ... " Phoebe trailed off, shaking her head in disappointment.

"I was so shocked to see the star gone. I told Zach so much about it."

"Oh, I know. It's awful. We had this horrible superstorm that damaged it and a lot of houses and businesses, too. The town looked devastated for a while, trees down everywhere. No power for days. Even the governor came."

"I heard about it a little from my dad. But driving down the mountain last night ... Pheebs, it just wasn't the same. It's like it wasn't our town."

"I know, everyone feels that way. Seeing our star lit above the valley ... " Phoebe looked off wistfully.

"My mother always said: *When you see the star, you'll know you're home.*"

Phoebe nodded. "And I remember on our sleepovers your mom would tell us stories about the star when she was a little girl."

"And we'd lie there and make wishes."

"And *you'd* call it *your* star, you little brat," Phoebe teased, giving her a little shove, "because we could see it from your pillow."

Hope shook her head, laughing. "Hey, I was little! And it did seem like it was my own star, right there out my bedroom window to wish on. It was so special." She sighed. "You know I've been telling Zach about it so much and now it's gone. I think he's really disappointed. He actually walked up there this morning all by himself to see if it could be fixed. Can you imagine?"

"Wow. He was on a mission."

"I wish there was something I could do about it."

"Well … " Phoebe said, smiling with raised eyebrows. "You are your mother's daughter. She'd never have given up. Maybe while you're here you could—"

Hope put a hand up, stopping her. "No, no, no. Don't start." Phoebe always had grand ideas. "I'm just here for a few days. I have an important article I need to write—"

"What! You're still writing! That's it, then, that's what you can do!"

"What are you talking about?"

"Write about it! Who better to write about the star than you?"

"Come on, that's crazy. How would I do that?"

"Oh, a little thing called a pen … and that lovely invention called paper? But I'll bet an ice cream soda you've got that newer device called a laptop!"

"Haha, funny. What I meant is that I'm leaving and … how on earth would I even start."

"Listen, now that things are kind of back to normal, just get people talking about what the star means to them. Get them excited so they'll donate money! We'll start a star fund."

"I appreciate your confidence, I really do. But my hands are full. And I want to make sure Zach gets all the Christmas he can while I've got him."

"Then you'll be here for the Hometown Holiday? Great, we can sure use your help."

Suddenly Zach was back, his basket filled with Pez, lollipops, Nerds and Chunkys.

"Can we, Mom? Can we stay for the Hometown Holiday?"

"Oh, Zach, I don't think—"

"But you told me how awesome it is," he pleaded, "and I've never seen a Santa Parade. And I want to take a horse and carriage ride."

"It's only next week," Phoebe chimed in. "Surely a few days extra won't matter. Remember how we used to stay up late, helping your mom with all the plans. It's in your genes, Hope!"

Zach was looking up at her with such a pleading expression. Her kid, who'd been through so much. Who was about to move again and wouldn't be at all happy about it.

She shook her head, laughing. "How can I so no to that face?"

"Yay!" Zach cried out, jumping up and down.

"But just for the first few days."

"Okay!"

Phoebe winked at Zach then led him to the counter where she dumped out his candy and began bagging it. When Hope pulled out her wallet, she held up a hand. "It's on the house.

On the condition that you think about coming to a Hometown Holiday meeting tonight at Mama's Café."

"I'll think about it … but I do have an entire attic to start plowing through."

"Thirty minutes."

"We'll see."

"I'll take it," Phoebe said, handing Zach his bag.

She turned to leave, realizing suddenly how much she'd missed Phoebe and her infectious optimism.

"Mom, can we go see Grandpa's store?" Zach asked once they were out on the sidewalk.

"Ummm, sure," she said, "but we need to cross to the other side."

They walked to the corner and crossed over to McClain's Hardware, which took up the entire corner of Plane Street. The store had a huge parking lot on the corner side and now, as it was every holiday of her life, half of the parking lot was filled with Christmas trees. Lights were strung above the trees and "Silver Bells" was playing on the speakers.

"Wow, look at all those trees!" Zach gushed as they neared.

They began walking through aisles of trees, Zach clearly in awe. Suddenly her dad appeared from behind a blue spruce.

"Grandpa," Zach called.

Her dad turned. "I thought I recognized that voice. Hello, Zach, Hope. I'm so glad you've come."

"Hi, Grandpa. I didn't know you sell Christmas trees," Zach said.

Her dad gave her a look. Of course, there was a lot Zach didn't know. How could he?

"We can't stay long, Dad. I really need to get started on the attic and Zach has some schoolwork he's got to get done."

"Well, how about Zach stays here with me? He can help me sell a tree or two. And you can get some work done."

"Can I, Mom?"

"And I'll make sure then he gets all his work done," her dad promised.

Hope hesitated, then nodded. Her father put an arm around Zach and led him away through another aisle of trees. "This here's a Frasier Fir, that one's a Douglas Fir, best Christmas smell ... " she heard him say as they disappeared among the evergreens.

CHAPTER 3

HOPE OPENED THE ATTIC DOOR, a cup of tea in her right hand, a small notepad and pen tucked in her pocket. How many times had she heard her mother say, *Oh, one day I've got to get organized and plow through that attic!* That day, like so many others for her mother, had never come.

At the top of the steps, she surveyed the big space. The old wooden floors and beams, the slightly tilting brick chimney climbing through the roof. There were endless boxes scattered haphazardly, old wardrobes, mirrors, a few trunks, and odds and ends. She turned to an alcove, turning on the light.

"Hello."

She jumped, spilling her tea. There was Ryan in a far corner beside a workhorse.

"Oh, you startled me," she said, "I forgot you were working up here. I'll try to stay out of your way."

"I'm just shoring up some roof beams. You should be fine," he said, picking up a board and laying it on the sawhorse. "Looks like you've got quite a chore ahead of you."

"Oh, my mother saved everything. Every fancy dress, every

paper I wrote, drawings, report cards, you name it."

"You're lucky."

"Your mother wasn't a saver?"

"I never knew my mother. She died when I was born. And my father ... well, I spent most of my youth in foster care. You learn to travel light."

"I'm so sorry."

He looked down at the board and began measuring. "No worries. They say you don't miss what you don't know."

"Is that why ... Christmas isn't your thing?"

He shrugged, his back still to her. "I'm just not into all the fuss."

She hesitated, then said, "What if—"

But her words were silenced by the sudden earsplitting whine of the electric saw slicing through the board. Their conversation was obviously over. Hope shook her head, slightly annoyed despite his heartbreaking admission about his childhood. Then she walked over to the biggest pile of boxes and sat on a trunk, surveying everything around her, trying to make a game plan. The saw stopped.

"What about you?" he asked suddenly. "How come you haven't been back in a while?"

She glanced over. He was looking at her. "It's complicated."

His eyebrows lifted and he nodded. She ripped open the box nearest to her. As he walked across the attic, she noticed the slight limp again.

"What happened to your leg?"

"That's complicated, too."

She couldn't tell if he gave her a smile or a smirk. He really was annoying, she decided.

"Are you really going to let the star go?"

"What is everyone's obsession with that star?" Now he sounded annoyed.

"Have you ever seen it lit over town? Across the valley?"

"No, the storm hit before I bought the property."

"Then you'll never understand."

"Seems like there's plenty of Christmas down here in the valley."

She shook her head. There was no point in getting into a debate with this man. She turned back to the box and sat on the floor beside it, lifting the top. Under some crumpled newspaper, she found an old wooden jewelry box. Oh, she remembered this box sitting on her mother's dresser throughout her childhood just full of treasures. How she'd loved opening all the little drawers. Trying on necklaces and bracelets and beautiful pins. Sometimes her mother would sit beside her and they'd play jewelry store, as she sold pieces to her mother for monopoly money and her mother made a big fuss of trying things on. As she got bigger, she longed to have her ears pierced so she could try all the earrings on, too.

She opened a few drawers now, holding up a string of pearls, a gold cross, then a crude bead bracelet she'd made in kindergarten, some of the paint worn off from her mother wearing it every day for she couldn't remember how long. There was no way she could just rush through this jewelry box and make decisions on each piece, there was too much. She set the jewelry box aside to bring downstairs for later.

She turned then to the big trunk she'd been sitting on and

knelt to open it. She gasped at what she found there sitting right on top. She pulled it out.

"I can't believe it! My mother's binder for the Hometown Holiday!" She began turning pages. Phoebe was right, no one did Christmas like her mother. How many times had she heard townspeople coming up to her mom on the street: *Alice, you've done it again! Best Hometown Holiday ever!*

Her heart ached looking at her mother's beautiful handwriting, all the little notes in blue ink in the typed margins of lists and instructions. Her mother's hands had touched these same pages that she was touching now. Tears filled her eyes. *Oh, Mom, I still can't believe you're not here.*

"You okay?"

She looked up, suddenly embarrassed, as she realized Ryan was right there, looking at her as he carried a board to the other side of the attic.

"Please, don't let me interrupt your work. I wouldn't want to bore you with this Christmas stuff."

His eyes widened at her dig but he said nothing and continued walking. It had come out harsh. Before she could apologize, the whine of the saw cut through the silence again. She turned back to the trunk, ordering herself to stop talking and focus. This was a bigger job than she'd anticipated. She had no idea how she was going to get this done in just a few days. There were too many memories. Too many items she couldn't just carelessly toss for donations or rubbish. And she couldn't waste time getting distracted. Or annoyed. Maybe she'd bring earbuds up next time and put on some soothing music. Because she had to focus, get this done, and get back to South Carolina as soon as she could. It seemed as though her whole life was riding on her Christmas article for the *Tribune*. And she hadn't even really started yet.

Daylight was fading by the time Hope went downstairs from the attic with yet another box of her own things from over the years, her back and knees aching from endless bending and crouching. She and Ryan managed to stay out of each other's way, and after a while, she simply turned on her music app on her phone to break the uncomfortable silence. It was on a Christmas station, of course. He said nothing.

As she got to the bottom of the stairs and stacked the box on top of a few others, the front door flew open and in walked her dad with Zach, who was bursting with excitement.

"Mom! Grandpa has seven different kinds of Christmas trees and there's one that's fifteen feet tall!"

"Wow, that's pretty big."

Her dad put his arm around Zach. "Turns out this young man is quite the salesman. He helped me sell more than a dozen trees."

"And Grandpa said I can go back and help tomorrow. I promise I'll get all my schoolwork done tonight."

Hope couldn't remember the last time she'd seen him this excited. Quite the opposite of the little boy who sullenly got in the car yesterday morning for the long trip.

"And Julia, I mean Mrs. Timbrook, said she could even help me. She was a teacher."

She looked at her dad, puzzled.

"Oh, Julia popped into the store for some extra lights for her house and … well, she did offer."

They were both looking at her in anticipation.

"Okay, I suppose that'll be fine. As long as your work gets done properly."

"It will, Mom."

Just then there was a knock at the door. Red walked over and opened it. There stood Phoebe with two men and two women behind her. Phoebe walked right in and stood in front of her.

"Hope, it's unanimous. We're here to take you to the meeting. We want you to head the Hometown Holiday, just like your mom used to do."

Hope's jaw dropped. They couldn't be serious. She looked from Phoebe to her father, whose eyes lit up with joy. And then she turned and looked at Zach, who was smiling from ear to ear. It felt like an ambush.

"Okay, you win, I'll go to the meeting," she said, taking her coat off the hook and slipping it on, "and I'll offer some suggestions. But … I can't promise anything other than that."

"Deal!" Phoebe said, with that smug look Hope remembered all too well.

And then they were off.

Mama's Café was all decorated for Christmas, with its signature Frank Sinatra music now playing his Christmas songs. Strings of colored Christmas lights hung from the ceilings and each table had a candle glowing in the middle. Hope's mouth watered the moment she walked in. Their pizza was legendary throughout her life and she hadn't had anything even close since living in the south. Tommy, the owner, and the rest of the staff all came over and gave her a hug before she sat with the committee at a big table already set up for them.

"Hope, let me formally introduce you to the gang. This is Rob from The Book Lover book shop near your dad's store. Then there's Lori, best dog groomer in town, Jane from the *Gazette*, and Norm from WRNJ."

Of course, she'd chatted with them all already on the way over, but each reached over now and shook her hand, murmuring how delighted they were she was on board. She didn't bother to dispute that. She'd settle things once and for all with Phoebe later on.

"Now where are we with our assignments," Phoebe said, opening a folder.

"Well, we've only got two stores besides mine taking part in the ice sculpture contest," said Rob from The Book Lover.

"Wait ... what?" Hope asked. "That's not possible. It used to be every store."

Phoebe looked at her, shaking her head. "I told you, Hope, things changed a lot after that storm. Some stores couldn't even reopen for months. I was one of them."

"Oh, Pheebs, I'm so sorry."

Norm held up a sheet of paper then. "The Santa Parade is going to be much smaller again, too. Just a few floats."

Phoebe was paging through her folder, then looked around. "Where on earth is Lauren? She's in charge of the Main Street decorations and they've got to start getting them up!"

"Here I am!"

They all turned to see a polished young blonde in a navy business suit and heels, carrying a briefcase and walking toward them. Hope was stunned to see Ryan just behind her. The two of them pulled up chairs. After a few greetings, Phoebe got right to the point.

"Lauren, where are we with the old Main Street decorations? They're supposed to go up in a few days. We're cutting it really close."

Lauren pursed her lips and then looked around the table, handing out photos from a big manila envelope she pulled from her briefcase. "Look, the vintage decorations may have to go up in stages because it's taking Ryan a bit longer on the repairs. Remember they've been in storage for decades and some of them need quite a bit of work."

"These decorations are beautiful, but they're metal and fragile," Ryan cut in. "Some of the detail is pretty intricate."

"Ryan, we're on a tight deadline," Lori, the dog groomer, chimed in. "We need to have some idea when they'll be ready."

He looked around the table. "Do you guys want it fast, or do you want it right?"

There was a long silence. Hope's eyes were riveted to a color photo in her hand. "Oh, I haven't seen these since I was just a little girl."

"All the newer ornaments were also destroyed in that storm," Phoebe explained to her. "Luckily we found these old ornaments from decades ago still in storage."

Hope held up her photo, looking at Ryan. "I remember these were strung with wire across the intersections all along

Main Street. Santa with his sleigh and reindeer looked just like he was really flying."

"Well, that one is nearly finished. Most of the antlers had broken off of the reindeer and the sled was in bad shape."

"Your work looks ... incredible." She almost hated admitting it. Something about him had just rubbed her the wrong way earlier, and she wasn't sure why. He'd kindly brought Zach home. He shared a sad history of his boyhood. And yet she felt as though he'd been a bit condescending about her love for Christmas. And yet here he was helping with the Hometown Holiday.

"Well thank you," he said with what she took as a smug smile.

"I'm sorry," Lauren said, suddenly zeroing in on her, "and you are?"

Hope extended a hand across the table. "Hope Reynolds."

Lauren took it and squeezed hard. "Lauren Adams."

"Lauren is vice-president of the Chamber of Commerce and has been pitching in since her boss hurt his back," Phoebe explained, then turned to Lauren. "Hope is Alice McClain's daughter."

"Alice was in charge of the Hometown Holiday for nearly three decades," said Jane from the *Gazette*.

"And Hope's agreed to take over, Lauren, so you're free to go back to running the Chamber full-time," Phoebe quickly added.

She wanted to jump in and vehemently deny what Phoebe said, but the fake smile Lauren gave her shut her down. There was something ... disingenuous about her. How could she let this woman take her mother's place?

"Well, gang, we've got a long way to go so let's all really push hard, especially with getting more participation. We'll meet again in a few days. I'll text everyone the details."

As they all got up from the table, Ryan walked over to Hope.

"I guess I shouldn't be surprised to see you here," he said.

"Well, I'm certainly surprised to see you here since Christmas isn't your thing."

He gave her a crooked smile, shaking his head. "It's a job. That's all."

Hope bit her tongue as he walked away with Lauren. Phoebe gathered her things and came over. "What's with you two?"

"Nothing," she said, pulling on her coat. "Nothing at all."

They sat in Phoebe's car in her dad's driveway, both of them silent.

"It's not good," Hope finally said.

"No, it's not. Three floats in the parade? That's pathetic."

"And my dad's not even one of them?"

"Hope, he hasn't participated in a long time. I don't think his heart's been in it since you left."

"I didn't realize that, but please, Pheebs, no more guilt trips, okay? I've got enough guilt already for ten people with everything I've got going on."

"I'm sorry."

"And ambushing me like that? That wasn't fair. You have

44

no idea how crazy my life is right now."

"Listen, you seem really stressed and don't seem to have time for anything that's fun. All those years we helped your mom? You loved it!"

She couldn't argue with that. Because she couldn't remember the last time she wasn't stressed. Or had actually had fun. When she was young her favorite time of year was the weeks going into Christmas. Her Mom was like a whirlwind of excitement and joy and she always wanted to be a part of it all. "I think that was the thing that made her happiest."

"Remember how beautiful she looked at the Jingle Ball every year in her red velvet cape and her gorgeous white velvet gown underneath it with the white furry muff? She looked like a snow queen."

Hope remembered thinking she looked as though she stepped right out of the pages of her fairy tale books.

"I didn't tell you but I found my mom's Hometown Holiday notebook. It details everything, including exactly where those vintage decorations and ornaments used to go. She also had lists of everything, including everyone who donated items to help with the events."

"See!" Phoebe said, reaching over and shaking her. "It's meant to be! And Hope, now you can give those memories to Zach!"

They sat in silence for a long moment. Hope looked out the car window, up toward Buck Hill and the dark empty space where the star used to shine. Then she looked at her house, the Christmas lights twinkling outside, the inside lit up so cozy. She could almost imagine her mother in there, cookies baking

45

in the oven, her binder on the counter as she drank a cup of peppermint tea and hummed a Christmas carol. These were the weeks she never stopped, making sure they had the best Christmas each year. Just as she made sure the town had the best Hometown Holiday. *For you, my darling,* she used to say to Hope.

She turned to Phoebe. "I'll do it. I'll—"

Phoebe grabbed her before she could finish speaking and hugged her tight. "You won't regret this, Hope."

"Listen, though," she said, pulling away, "I'll get it started for you, but I can't stay for all of it. Okay?"

"Okay, but what about the star? Would you consider writing about it for a fundraiser?"

"You don't quit!" she said, almost laughing because Phoebe was the same as when they were in high school. "I can't, I'm sorry. The article I told you I need to write? It's to hopefully save my job with the city newspaper I work for."

"Oh. I'm sorry, I didn't realize that."

"Not to mention the house I'm renting sold, so Zach and I have to move again after the holidays. And he loves it where we are, our neighbors, his friends, his school. He's had a tough time since … my divorce."

"Oh, Hope. I really am sorry. You do have a lot on your plate."

She sighed. It felt more like her plate was overflowing and drowning her.

"Don't get me wrong, I'm still heartbroken the star is gone. Especially seeing Zach disappointed and … oh my gosh, imagining him climbing up that mountain, cold and shivering and not really knowing where he was going. And he'd never even been in snow before! It just kills me."

"He seems like a really good kid, Hope. I'm sure he'll be fine."

"He is." Just then she saw a light go out in the living room. "I'd better go. I want to tuck Zach in. And then the attic is calling me. I didn't realize just how much was up there."

"A lifetime of stuff," Phoebe said, softly.

"And a lifetime of memories."

Ryan Miller threw more logs into the woodstove. Within minutes the cold workshop began to warm up nicely. He picked up a board, ran his hand across the grain and inhaled the sweet scent of pine. He'd learned about woodworking when he was in high school. The shop teacher had told him he seemed to have a natural talent for working with wood. All he knew, though, was there was something peaceful about it. And it was gratifying to create something. Besides, for a little while he could get lost and forget about everything else, even back then.

This workshop was something he'd never even dreamed of. But it was already there when he saw the house, and though it wasn't in great shape, he knew it wouldn't take much to fix it up. Now the cracks in the siding had been filled in, he'd installed better windows, and even on a blustery winter day, it could maintain its heat. In a way, he loved it even more than the house.

It was late, it had been a long day, and his leg was throbbing. But his projects were piling up. And often he'd work before going to bed. Somehow it calmed his mind. Now he thought about the little boy, Zach, who'd made his way up here that morning. That was one gutsy kid. And then he pictured the mother, Hope, who happened to be Red's daughter. The kid was right, there was something sad about those gray eyes. Beautiful eyes, really. Stop, he warned himself, as he picked up the board. He wasn't about to get himself caught up in any of that. He'd built a good life here with his house, his workshop, and now a pretty good business going. That was enough. He didn't need complications. He'd already had enough of those to last two lifetimes.

Because Ryan Miller had learned all too often that it was best to guard your heart.

Hope sat on the attic floor in a puddle of light from several old lamps plugged in and turned on all around her. She was reading through the stacks of papers surrounding her. She'd just finished through her third-grade pile and needed to give her eyes a break, so she turned to a stack of photos that had been inside a big zip-lock bag. Here were her school photos. As she looked through them one by one, she saw herself year by year growing up: teeth missing and growing in, bangs cut then bangs gone, then braces for a few years. And there she was a freshman in high school, her face thinner, her ears finally pierced, and sophomore year with the twirling squad, holding a baton she'd been practicing with for years. And finally, her senior portrait, long brown hair curled so carefully by her mom, and looking so serious. Having been accepted to colleges and already nervous about going away. She could remember sitting there as Mr. Niper clicked away, thinking about the future ahead of her. Wondering if she'd really be a writer, as she always dreamed. Imagining falling in love, because though she dated a bit in high school, she'd never had a true first love.

Underneath the school portraits were the rest of her childhood pictures. Phoebe was there in so many of them. How had she let so many years go by? Until she heard that voice calling her name, she had no idea how much she'd missed her childhood best friend. Soul sisters, they'd always called themselves. No one knew her like Phoebe did.

Just then the college bells tolled eleven o'clock and she chided herself for taking too much time again caught up in the past. Like the jewelry box, she couldn't race through these photos. She'd simply have to fill another box to take home. But as she went to slide the photos back into the big zip-lock bag, they fell and a very old one landed by her foot. Her breath caught.

"Oh, Mom … " Tears flooded her eyes.

There was her mother all dressed up in her red velvet cape with the hood up, one hand inside the white fur muff, the other holding Hope's hand. Her father must have taken the picture because he wasn't in it. She couldn't have been more than seven, in her own red coat with a red beret, a little white muff like her mother's, and patent leather shoes. Her mother's face just beamed with joy.

"Oh, Mom, you were so beautiful."

She pulled the photo to her mouth and kissed her mother, then held it to her chest for a long moment, tears streaming down her cheeks. When she was finally able to compose herself, she slowly put the picture on top of her mother's Hometown Holiday notebook to bring downstairs. There wasn't much left in this trunk and she forced herself to continue, to feel as if she accomplished something this evening.

She dug the last pile out of the trunk, began sorting more quickly, and then gasped again as she stared at a piece of lined composition paper filled with her first attempts at cursive handwriting. Shaking her head, she smiled, remembering how she'd grip the pen so hard that her hand would hurt. She began to read aloud. *The Christmas Star by Hope McClain, Grade 4. In our town every Christmas we have a star lit on top of a mountain called Buck Hill and it looks like it's floating up in the sky. I'm the luckiest girl in town because I can see it from my pillow when I go to sleep. My Mom says the star stands for hope and because of that she and my dad named me Hope.*

Her throat began to ache again trying to contain her tears. She continued reading silently, then picked up the photo once more. "Oh, Mom, I think maybe I've lost hope. I feel like a failure with Zach. I want to give him the real home he deserves. I need to write the best article of my life. I … "

It was hard to continue. The last time she felt this defeated was when Drew told her he was leaving her. She got up and walked over to the attic window tucked under an eave, and looked up at Buck Hill, dark in the distance.

"I need to feel hope again."

CHAPTER 4

IT WAS A CLEAR AND frigid morning as Hope turned onto Buck Hill Lane, the snow-draped trees shimmering in the early sunshine. She'd never actually been up here before and now she imagined Zach trudging up the steep, winding road and her heart melted. He no doubt completely missed the *No Trespassing* signs high on the trees.

She left him in the kitchen earlier with Julia, who'd shown up with a delicious French toast casserole, and then offered to help him get started with the day's schoolwork to give Hope some much-needed free time for all she needed to get done. After debating with herself for a few moments, Hope texted Ryan.

As she reached the top of the lane, there was a big clearing with a house and an outbuilding beside it. On the other side of the clearing were the remains of her beloved Christmas Star. She got out of her car and just stood there, looking up at the twisted pieces of metal and wires hanging from the top half. The bottom half wasn't bad, you could still see the outline of the star, and some of the lights were still attached. But all in all, it was just a giant mess.

She heard a door close and turned to see Ryan coming out of what she assumed was his workshop beside the house. A black and white dog trailed behind him.

"It's pretty bad," she admitted.

"I'm sorry, I know it means a lot to you."

"And to the town." She looked at him then. "How can you just leave it like this? It's so … sad to see."

"I'm not. I'm taking it down in the spring."

For a moment she couldn't even speak, imagining the star just gone. Forever.

"Are you serious?" she finally asked. "You'll be tearing down a piece of this town's history. Not to mention the memories of so many people."

He looked up, surveying the damage, shaking his head. "I don't think I have a choice."

"I'm not so sure about that," she said, instantly regretting her words when he looked at her with a puzzled frown.

"What do you mean by that?" he challenged.

"Nothing. Just that people will be very upset and probably not hide the fact." She took a deep breath. "Anyway, I have the original list of the decorations and where they should go, as I said in my text. I thought it might help you to see where they go exactly since you'll also be hanging them, right?"

"Yes, that's right. Come on in, then," he said, leading her to the workshop.

She walked in behind him and as he went over to a tool rack, her eyes surveyed the room. It was all wood beams and walls, but the lighting overhead was good and a woodstove blazed in the corner. Tools and workbenches were against one wall and in the center was a big work table. Various Christmas decorations were scattered about and her eyes suddenly landed on Santa with his sleigh and reindeer against a far wall. She walked over.

"That's ready to be hung," he said.

"But ... I thought you said—"

"I stayed up after the meeting last night to finish it. It seemed important to you, so I thought it should go up first."

She looked at him, clearly puzzled. And stunned. He obviously thought she was obsessed with Christmas and seemed annoyed by it. And yet he stayed up late fixing her favorite old decoration from her childhood. She couldn't figure him out.

"It was my favorite when I was a little girl. Thank you that was ... thoughtful. Since it's just another job."

He gave her a satisfied smile that might have been a smirk. "I take my work seriously. Even if it's for Christmas."

She walked around the big table, telling herself not to let him annoy her. He seemed to have a knack for it. She noticed then the old sled on the workbench where he was standing.

"Wow, is that an old Flexible Flyer?"

He nodded.

"I had that same sled when I was little." She walked over to look at it more closely.

"Zach didn't seem to know what it was. He's never been sleigh riding?"

"We live in the south," she said in defense. "There isn't snow, so ... no, he hasn't been."

"Still. Hasn't he been up here in the winter?"

She opened her mouth to speak but a sudden knock stopped her and a second later the door opened. In walked Lauren, heading right to Ryan with a big smile until she noticed Hope.

"Oh, hello, Hope. Hi Ryan. I was just coming to check on ... " but she stopped speaking suddenly as her eyes landed on Santa and his sleigh, her eyes widening. She turned and put a hand on Ryan's arm. "Oh, my gosh, you did this last night after the meeting? You are amazing!"

Hope cleared her throat. It was obvious Lauren had designs on Ryan and something about Lauren's confidence and less than genuine smiles reminded her of Drew's latest girlfriend, Marisa, who she met the last time Drew took Zach for a weekend.

"Well, I'd better go. I'll just leave you the list."

She pulled the list from her bag and put it on the table. Ryan walked over to take it, Lauren following just a few inches behind.

"By the way," Lauren said, now looking at the list over Ryan's shoulder, "I'm happy to turn the Hometown Holiday over to you. It'll free me up to give Ryan more help here."

Hope simply nodded and turned to the door.

"Wait," Ryan called out, "I thought you said you wanted to go over the list with me?"

She smiled, a little too sweetly. "Oh, I think you guys can figure it out."

She opened the door, walked outside, and let out a long breath. She didn't like disliking someone and now she chastised herself about Lauren. She knew nothing about her and shouldn't judge her. So what if she seemed possessive of Ryan? It was none of her business. As for Ryan, the man was a true paradox, uncaring and annoying one moment, and then thoughtful the next. But again, what did it matter?

She walked to her car, then looked up at the star for a long moment, imagining it up close like this, shining as she'd never seen it. As it had for more than 75 years, filling the entire mountaintop with light. Year after year calling out to the people in town with its message of love and hope. Now it was so damaged and looked so sad. As if it were defeated, as she sometimes felt. She could have cried.

And that was, after all, why it mattered.

When she got out of her car a few minutes later in her dad's driveway, Hope could hear Zach laughing. She walked over to the open garage door. One bay held her father's car and in the other was the old flatbed truck her dad owned for as long as she could remember.

"Mom!"

Zach came running to her just as her father came from behind the truck.

"Mom, I'm gonna help grandpa make a float for the parade!"

"Wow, that's ... exciting!" She looked at her father, puzzled. "They told me last night you haven't ... " She shook her head, not wanting to say more in front of Zach.

"Well, I can't let Zach go to the parade and not even be in it, can I?" her father said, with the first real smile since she arrived.

Hope sighed. Things were getting more complicated by the minute.

"Zach," her dad said, "can you run into the kitchen and get me the tape measure in the drawer next to the stove?"

"Sure," he said, racing into the house.

"I hear you agreed to head the Hometown Holiday," her dad said now, with a little catch in his voice. "You know your mom would be so happy and proud."

"I know, Dad, but I'm just helping to get it started. I can't stay. I was clear with them about that."

"Honey, Zach is really excited about the float. He has a surprise he's planning for you, and it was really all his idea. I hope you can stay for that, at least."

"I'm glad he's excited."

"He's a good boy. You've done an amazing job despite—"

She put her hand up, stopping him. "Please, let's not go into all of that, okay Dad? I know he deserved better."

Her father sighed. "So did you."

She could feel her eyes pinching, fighting tears. "We're doing okay, really. And yes, I did kind of promise him we'll be here for the parade. So, whatever his surprise is, we won't miss it. But then we do have to get right back home. And now ... I've got to work on an article, then get back to the attic."

She started walking to the house, then turned suddenly. "Dad, about the star. Isn't it in the deed or something that the owner of the house on Buck Hill has to allow the star to remain there? And that it has to be lit each Christmas?"

"I believe so, Honey. As far as I know. Why?"

She hesitated. "Nothing, just ... wondering." Then Zach was running back out of the house. "Listen, buddy, I've got to get some work done, then how about we go into town? We're going to start hanging the Hometown Holiday decorations all along Main Street."

"Okay, Mom, that sounds awesome. But no more coming into the garage, okay?"

"Aye, aye, sir," she said with a smile and a salute.

She watched them go back into the garage and a moment later, the garage door slowly closed. When was the last time she'd seen Zach so enthusiastic? Not even complaining about his schoolwork. It touched her heart to hear it in his voice, especially how he seemed to be bonding with her father. With his occasional visits and too frequent cancelations, Drew had never given Zach that same chance. He was always too busy. Or something else was more important.

Her son really had deserved better. And so had she.

Hope sat on her old bed with her computer on her lap, surrounded by pages and notes. She began typing: *Christmas in The City*, hesitated, then continued. *What makes Christmas in the city so special?* She sat there, waiting for inspiration, drumming her fingers on the edge of the keyboard, thinking. Willing something to come to her. She began again: *There is nothing like the lights of the city to ...* she deleted that. *Who doesn't love looking in department store windows and ...* shaking her head, she deleted that, too.

What happened to all of the ideas that had been percolating

in her brain on the long drive north, while she was listening to audiobooks on fueling creativity? It was like they vanished the moment she arrived here. The moment she got pulled back into her old life. And the magic of Christmas in Hackettstown.

She closed her eyes, sighing. She never had trouble zeroing in on a topic. How often had she turned in articles with insane deadlines? She could always be counted on. And now, the most important article she'd write, the one that could save her job … she was blank.

Glancing out the window, she saw the sun was already high, the morning ticking by way too quickly. Her eyes then landed on the sheet of composition paper from fourth grade that also sat on the bed beside her. She picked it up and slowly she read her words again, a tiny smile beginning. Her little fingers had written these sentences. Her little heart had been filled with so much joy, and hope. When she finished reading, she sat there as her mind began to hum, and an idea began to sing. Quickly she began to type: *Once upon a time, there was a little girl who believed anything was possible, especially at Christmas. She had her own Christmas Star to wish upon … "*

Just then her cell rang. She wanted to ignore it, to not stop the flow of her idea. But she quickly glanced at her phone and saw it was Lily. She picked up, hoping maybe it was good news.

"How's it going up there in the wintry north?" Lily asked in her classic southern drawl.

"Oh, Lil, you have no idea. My head is spinning."

"What on earth is going on?"

"Well, I thought I'd pack up the attic and head home in a few days, as I planned. But now … I'm involved with the

Hometown Holiday. And later today I have to cajole some merchants into participating in the ice sculpture contest."

"Whoa," Lily laughed. "And what about Zach?"

"Actually, Zach is having a great time. He absolutely loves the snow. And right now, he's helping my dad make a float for the Santa Parade. It's a surprise he's planning for me. Then this afternoon, I'm taking him to watch Ryan hang the Christmas decorations along Main Street."

"Who's Ryan?"

"Oh, he's just a handyman fixing up my dad's roof. And apparently volunteering for the Hometown Holiday decorations."

"Handyman, hmmmm?" Lily giggled.

"Don't start, Lil. How many times have I told you, I have no time for a guy, despite you trying to fix me up every other week."

"Is he cute?"

"Annoying. And not my type."

"Hope, I don't think you have any idea what your type is anymore. When's the last time you were even on a date?"

"Lil," she warned in a serious tone, "you know Zach comes first. Maybe when he's older. He puts up with enough of that from his father and his revolving door of girlfriends."

"Okay, okay. So, tell me, how's that article coming for the *Tribune*?"

Sighing, Hope looked at her screen. "It's not really yet. Every time I try to write, it's like my mind goes blank. I'm playing with something now, but it's for something else entirely."

"Ooooh, what else?"

"Just something personal. More like journaling. But tell me, because I got excited when I saw your call, is the sale going through? Any chance it isn't?"

"Well … so far it all looks good. I'm sorry."

"Boo. I was afraid of that. Any new rental listings? I'm starting to get really nervous with the timing."

"Not yet, listings are always slow during the holidays. But get that article done so you can keep your job. Then you can buy a house instead of renting the next house! And stay put with Zach."

"Listen, the other two writers are really good. One guy's been with the paper at least a decade more than me and people love his style of humor. The really young gal, she's only been with us a few years at best, but she seems to have her finger on the millennials and we need to grow our readership, so … it's going to be tough."

"Oh, Hope, I've got my fingers and toes crossed for you. And if I have to … I'll cross my eyes, too," Lily laughed.

Hope smiled, but couldn't manage a laugh. "I may need more than that. Writing jobs are getting harder and harder to find. They're shrinking because so much is online now. And so much is free on the internet."

"Well, I still prefer a real newspaper. And a real book."

"So do I. But listen Lil, I really am starting to get nervous. What if I can't find anything by the time the closing happens and we have to be out?"

"I won't let that happen. We still have a little time, so just try to stay hopeful."

She looked out the window at the top of Buck Hill. "I will."

✳

Later that day, Hope and Zach walked into town with her dad. Main Street was bustling with activity as they neared Grand Avenue, where a small crowd gathered. She noticed Ryan's black pickup truck parked by the corner and a giant step ladder beside it. As they got closer, Zach began to pull her in his excitement.

"Wow, Mom, look up!"

It was then she saw that Ryan was at the top of the big ladder, putting the finishing touches on hanging Santa, his reindeer and sleigh from a wire strung across the intersection. They watched along with the crowd as he adjusted the back of the sleigh for a while so that it hung slightly lower than the reindeer. Finally, Ryan began climbing down the ladder.

"It looks good, Ryan, but … " she called out, trying to catch him while he was still up there. He obviously hadn't heard her, though when he reached the bottom and stepped onto the sidewalk, he came right over.

"It looks good, but what?" he asked, frowning.

"Oh, I didn't think you heard me. I actually brought the picture of exactly how it used to hang," she said, pulling the old photo out of her purse, "kind of on more of an angle, like this."

She handed Ryan the photo, pointing to what she meant. He nodded up toward the sleigh. "It is on an angle."

"The left side needs to be higher, so it looks like he's flying up into the sky. This looks more like—"

"I think it's fine the way it is!"

They both turned to see Lauren walking their way. Lauren

gave Ryan a syrupy smile.

Hope backed away with her photo and began nodding in agreement. "You know what? It is fine. No worries."

Ryan looked at her for a long moment. Then he turned and moved the ladder to the first reindeer in front of Santa, which was Rudolph, and somehow hitched it higher on the wire. Everyone continued watching, Lauren, too, as Ryan continued moving the ladder to adjust each reindeer.

"Hope is that you!" she heard suddenly and turned to see Mr. and Mrs. Hodge, Phoebe's parents, strolling by. They stopped to give her a hug. "We haven't seen you in so long!" Mr. Hodge said. "And this must be your little boy!"

She put an arm around Zach, who smiled shyly. "Yes, this is Zach, my amazing son."

"Well, young man, you must be so proud of your mom, taking over the Hometown Holiday like her mom used to do. And Phoebe told us," Mrs. Hodge said, now looking at Hope "that you're writing a piece for the *Gazette* to get the star lit again. We are so happy! We all miss the star!"

Hope's jaw dropped open in shock. Her dad's eyes widened and a moment later he was grinning ear to ear. And Zach was looking at her in surprise.

"Christmas just isn't the same without our star," Mrs. Hodge went on. "And you're such a beautiful writer."

"Oh, no, I—"

But Mr. Hodge cut right in, thinking she was denying her gift. "Your mother is too modest, Zach. Do you know there wasn't a dry eye at high school graduation after she read her essay about believing in dreams. She was quite inspiring."

"You know," said Ruth, from the Hometown Holiday committee, who was standing nearby, "if it wasn't for the star, I wouldn't even be living here!"

"Is that so?" Mrs. Hodge asked.

"Absolutely. I was pregnant and we were looking for our first house but had no luck at all. Then we had one more home to look at in this little town we'd never been to. As we started driving down the mountain it was already getting dark and I saw all the lights across the valley and then ... suddenly there was a beautiful star lit up across the sky and shining over this town. It was like it was calling us home."

"That's what my mother always said," Hope told them. "*When you see the star, you'll know you're home.*"

"That she did," Red added, his eyes shining.

"Everyone in town has a story about our star," said Norm from WRNJ.

"Hope, if you write something I will definitely put it in the *Gazette*," Jane from the newspaper added. "But you'll have to do it fast so there's enough time to get it printed and raise money to get the star lit by Christmas."

"You can do this, Hope!" Mrs. Hodge said, clapping her hands with excitement. "And your mom would be so proud."

Hope looked at Zach, who'd heard every word of this, now staring at her expectantly. She opened her mouth to say she couldn't possibly, that there wasn't enough time, and she had to leave, but ... no words came out.

"You should do it, Mom," Zach said finally. Her dad nodded his approval.

Before she could even respond, Ryan was suddenly standing

there, looking at her expectantly. "There," he said, nodding up to the wire, "how's that? Enough of an angle?"

She realized he wanted her approval on the Santa and sleigh. He hadn't heard anything about her writing to bring the star back. She looked up at Santa in his sleigh, with his eight reindeer pulling him up to the sky. Zach gave Ryan a thumbs up as she said, "It's perfect. Thank you."

Ryan smiled and gave her a little bow. Lauren sidled up to him again. "Fantastic once again, Ryan."

To prevent the conversation from veering back to the star, Hope quickly turned to Zach and her dad. "Zach, listen, we've got to go hit all the stores and convince them to get on board with the ice sculpture contest for the Hometown Holiday, okay?"

"That sounds boring. Can I go to Grandpa's store again?"

"Sounds like a grand idea," her dad said immediately.

"Are you sure? I know you need to work, too, Dad. This is your busy season."

"I told you this young man here is a natural-born sales-man," he said, putting an arm around Zach.

"Just like my dad!"

Hope and her dad gave each other a long look.

An hour later, Hope had already gotten a "no" and a "maybe" about the ice sculpture contest from two of the store owners she visited. Then she went to Harper's Bakery, its front windows filled with delicious cookies, cakes, and Christmas treats. There was an entire shelf of gingerbread houses and she reminded herself that she still wanted to make one with Zach.

The little bell rang when she opened the door, a sound from her childhood that heralded frosted cupcakes or her favorite everything bagel. Mr. Harper, she was surprised to see, was now completely gray. He ambled behind the counter in his white apron, but as he looked up, his eyes widened, and he smiled.

"Hope McClain! Is that really you?"

"Hi Mr. Harper, and it's Hope Rey—"

"I haven't seen you in years! I was just the other day telling my niece about you, best summer worker I ever had."

"Oh my gosh, Mr. Harper, that seems like a million years ago. And I did love working here. Though I think I gained another five pounds each summer of high school."

"Aaah! You were just a sapling to start with anyway." He came around the counter then to give her a hug. "So, I hear you're going to get our star up and lit again, that's wonderful."

How was it possible, she wondered, that everyone in town thought this? But she knew, of course. Phoebe!

"Actually, Mr. Harper, I'm here to see if I can't talk you into doing one of your fabulous ice sculptures for the Hometown Holiday again. Remember when you did that amazing gingerbread man? Why, I think you won three years in a row, isn't that right?"

"Oh yes," he said, leading her to one of the tables. "I do remember. But I wanted to tell you a little story about the star you might want to use in that article."

"But I'm not really—"

"And then you can tell me more about your ice sculpture

ideas because I'm a little rusty. I haven't done one in years."

There was no way out of this, listening to the stories everyone had of the star, just like in the last few stores. So, she followed Mr. Harper to a little table and sat down and listened as he told her about when he was a little boy and the stories he'd heard about how the star began.

CHAPTER 5

IT WAS NEARLY DARK WHEN Hope walked into her dad's house, exhausted from having to cajole the shopkeepers to agree to participate in the ice sculpture contest. And from having to first listen to the endless stories about the star. Not that they weren't heartwarming and moving, all of them. But she was fried.

She was just hanging up her coat in the foyer when her cell rang. She pulled it out of her purse and grimaced when she saw who it was. She didn't have a good feeling.

"Hello, Drew."

"Hey, I'm about to board a flight. I've got a sudden meeting in Asia, but I wanted to let you know there's been a slight change of plans."

She stood there, listening to the sounds of the airport in the background and trying to keep her cool. She knew what was coming. She could almost have predicted it.

"Please don't tell me you're canceling on Zach again."

"No, no," he said, nearly out of breath as if he were

running to catch his flight. "I'm sending him a ticket to meet us in L.A. because—"

"No!" she interrupted.

"Hope, listen, Marisa has to—"

"No, Drew. He's nine. I am not letting him fly across the country alone because you're too busy, or your girlfriend can't—"

"Whoa! Whoa! That's not fair, and there's no reason to get angry. Kids fly alone all the time. There are plenty of safety measures in place."

"No, Drew. Not my kid." She took a long breath, trying to slow her heart from galloping in her chest. "And what's not fair is the kind of father you are to him. Please fix this. And please don't disappoint him yet again."

She cut him off then, hanging up before he could say anything further. She was so tired of playing nice, always trying to keep things on an even keel, always so afraid it might end up spoiling something for her son. She turned to put her phone back into her purse. And there was Ryan, standing where he must've stopped halfway down the stairs, looking at her.

"I'm sorry, I was just coming down and … " he shrugged. "Are you okay?"

"Yes … no. I could just scream. That was Zach's dad. He's supposed to be taking him to Hawaii for Christmas but … the excuses are starting. And unfortunately, I know where this is probably going."

"I'm sorry." He came down to the foyer and put his toolbox down.

"This is what he does. Builds up Zach's hopes, changes the

68

plans a few times, then bails or disappoints him somehow. And somehow there's always a new girlfriend at the heart of it."

"Zach seems like a really good kid."

"He really is. But lately ... he's been acting out a bit. Like disappearing and going to find the star without telling anyone. He'll be devastated if his dad bails on him again."

Ryan nodded. "I'm sorry. I know what that feels like. My father was in and out of my life, but never really much of a father and ... I acted out, too." He gave a little laugh. "I actually got myself into a bit of trouble when I was older and then ... I enlisted."

"You were in the military?"

"Marines. I got the structure I needed and, well, the family I never really had. But Zach, he has *you.*"

She stared at him in surprise at these revelations.

"You're a good mother, Hope. Anyone can see that."

Here he was, surprising her again with empathy. After annoying her just a few hours ago.

"Thanks. I've tried. I've had to be not just mom, but dad, too, since Drew left when Zach was three. I'm the one who actually taught him how to hit a ball with a bat, and how to hook a fishing pole with a disgusting worm." She gave a little shiver of disgust and they both laughed. "But I can't give him the one thing he really wants. His dad. Or a real home of our own."

"Doesn't he pay child support?"

"Oh, he got a high-powered attorney and managed to get away with the minimum. And no alimony on top of it, so ... it's not so easy being a single mother in today's world."

Ryan was looking at her intensely and she dropped her

eyes, embarrassed suddenly at how much she'd shared. "I'm sorry, I didn't mean to get so personal." She shook her head to clear the mood. "Anyway, I'd better get to work, I have——"

The front door opened suddenly and Zach burst in with her dad, just like he did the day before.

"Mom! Guess what? We got a real tree! The biggest one Grandpa had!"

"What?" She couldn't help but laugh, he was so excited.

"Uh, Ryan, would you mind giving me a hand? Or three?" her dad asked with a laugh.

Ryan gave her one last look, nodded, then headed out the door with Zach and her dad.

Hope and Zach stood in the family room watching Ryan and her dad carrying the tree in.

"It's ginormous," Zach exclaimed.

And it was. It was bigger than any of the trees her father had brought home her entire childhood. Now she ran over to help, seeing her dad's face all red with exertion.

"I hope our tree stand is big enough," her dad said with a laugh as they leaned the tree in the corner of the room.

"I'll go get it, Red," Ryan offered. "I saw it in the attic. Hope would you ... ?"

She came around to his side of the tree to hold it up there, but it slipped and as it started to go down, they both grabbed for it together, their faces just inches apart. For a moment their eyes connected. And for that moment she found it hard to breathe. His eyes were such a clear blue, staring at her so intensely. She looked away first.

"We never had a real tree," Zach said, breaking into the moment. "My dad is allergic so we couldn't have one when he came to visit."

"But we've had some beautiful trees," she said, careful to look anywhere but at Ryan.

"Yeah, but they weren't real," Zach insisted.

"Zach," her dad said, "why don't you go up in the attic and help Ryan. Maybe you can bring down some ornaments, too, so we can start decorating."

He was gone in a flash, following Ryan up the stairs. Her father walked back across the room to where she stood making sure the tree didn't fall.

"Honey, I know you have to leave soon, but I have an idea. Why don't you come back for Christmas?"

She hesitated. Her dad looked so hopeful. "I really can't. I have too much going on back home."

"This will always be your home, Hope." There was no missing the catch in her father's voice.

"Dad, we have to move soon and I don't even know where we'll be going yet."

They turned then as Ryan came back carrying a bin and the tree stand, Zach behind him with a small box. Hope knelt at the bottom of the tree as Ryan, with a little help from her dad, lifted the tree and set it in the stand. They all stood back to admire it.

"It's perfect, isn't it, Zach?" her dad asked, obviously pleased with himself.

"It's the best. Mom, can we take a picture so I can show

Jackson how big it is when we get back? He won't believe it!"

"Of course, Honey."

Then Zach opened the small box he'd carried down from the attic. "Look what I found in the attic, Mom," he said, picking up a star studded with crystals. "Maybe we can wish on this one instead of the one that got broken?"

He handed her the star and she held it, unable to speak for a moment. Afraid she might cry. His little face looked up at her with such hope, and she imagined all those wishes he'd been saving. "That's a great idea, Zach. I love it."

"Can we decorate the tree now? Can Ryan help, too?" He looked at Ryan pleadingly.

Ryan hesitated, glanced at her, then said, "Sure, I can take a little time away from the roof."

"Great," she said, smiling at Zach.

Her father looked at them a moment. "Well, I've got to finish up a few things at the store, so you can surprise me when I get home later. You know, Zach, your mom and Grandmother Alice used to get the tree all decorated, and then we'd all light it together when I'd get home from the store, right, Honey?"

"Yes, we did."

It was as if he was reading her mind. From the moment they'd carried the tree in, an ache for her mom grew within her. Not the everyday feeling of loss that she was used to now. This felt as if she'd disappeared a moment ago from this room, to get another strand of lights or a few Christmas cookies to hold them over, and you could still smell her floral perfume or hear her voice. *I'll be back in just a moment.*

How could they be doing this without her? Right now, her

mother would be humming Christmas carols, or heating up hot chocolate for them, exclaiming over each ornament as they took them out of the boxes and placed them on the tree. Then she'd be so excited for their own "grand illumination" when her dad came home. *Red, come see, I think we've outdone ourselves this year.* Of course, she said that every year, it seemed.

They were the kind of memories she always wanted to give Zach. Home. Tradition. But they'd moved so much, first with Drew's job, then after he left. And it was hard to keep a tradition going when each holiday was different because of Drew's ever-changing demands.

"Mom?" Zach said loudly.

She looked over to see both her son and Ryan looking at her with puzzled expressions.

"Oh, sorry, just caught up in memories for a moment. Okay now, here's the plan. The lights have to go on first. We have to wrap the trunk with strands of light from the bottom to the top. And when that's done, we do the branches."

They both looked at her blankly. Of course, she and Zach always had a pre-lit artificial tree, not that she ever felt there were enough lights. But she had to do this tree right. The way her mother would have. It was unthinkable to do it any other way.

"Seriously?" Ryan asked then. "How on earth do you wrap lights around the trunk."

"Very carefully," she said with a little laugh, remembering her mother donning her gardening gloves to keep her hands from getting stabbed by needles. "Don't worry, it's a one-person job and I'm taking it. In the meantime, how about you guys go back upstairs and get the rest of the lights and ornaments. We've got a lot of Christmas tree to cover here."

It was the first time she'd ever undertaken the tedious job of wrapping the lights around the trunk, weaving the wire around and around, between branches, and it was backbreaking. But she knew it would give the tree a depth and beauty it couldn't get with just lit branches alone. As she got higher, Ryan brought down the step ladder, then stood beside her in case she slipped, despite her assurances she was fine. When she finished her arms ached and she had a new appreciation for what her mother went through each year. But for her mother, no job was too difficult to make Christmas perfect.

Ninety minutes later it was already dark outside as the last of the ornaments went on and Hope handed the star to Zach. Ryan moved the ladder closer to the tree and held onto Zach as he climbed, then reached as far as he could to place the star on the very top. Ryan hadn't said much as they decorated, and Hope wondered what was going through his head. As Zach came down the ladder, they heard the front door close.

"Well, looks like I'm back just in time," her dad said, standing in the doorway and unzipping his coat. And then she noticed Julia just beside him.

"Grandpa, I put the star all the way on top," Zach said.

"I can see. You did a great job."

"Okay, is everybody ready?" Hope asked, walking behind the tree and picking up the plug.

"Ready," they all called out.

"Okay, turn all the other lights off." Suddenly the room was completely dark. Hope bent down and felt along the wall for the outlet, then slipped the plug in. The room suddenly filled with amber light.

"Wow," Zach exclaimed, as he looked up at the tree.

"A thousand lights altogether," Hope said, coming around to see it for herself.

"Your mom would have loved it," her dad said. "You've done her proud, all of you."

"Oh, yes, it's every bit as lovely, Hope," Julia said.

Hope turned, looking for Ryan, realizing he wasn't there. Just then he came back into the room and slowly looked up at the tree, from bottom to top, squinting slightly, and with a look she couldn't read.

"What do you think, Ryan? Worth all that effort?" She couldn't help nudging him a bit.

"It's ... really quite something." And then he smiled. "And you were right about wrapping the trunk."

She wondered if it was painful for him, seeing a happy family moment like this, a Christmas tradition when he'd never really had any. She felt bad, then, for her little dig.

"You must have all worked up quite an appetite," Julia said. "I brought over a lasagna and some brownies for dessert."

"I love lasagna," Zach exclaimed. "And brownies!"

They all laughed.

"Ryan, stay for dinner, won't you?" Her dad asked.

Ryan looked surprised and then nodded. "Sure. Thank you."

It was the first time Ryan sat for a family dinner since ... he couldn't remember when. Oh, friends from the service sometimes invited him over from time to time, and sometimes to try to fix him up. But those were all a long time ago. At first, he felt a little uncomfortable sitting with Red and his family. But eventually, he found himself relaxing. Zach had them laughing with his crazy riddles and the food was incredible. It was also the first time since he'd met her that Hope seemed to finally let go of whatever seemed to be eating away at her. He sensed it was more than her ex.

At the end of the meal, he stood when Hope did, to help clear the dessert plates. "That was a delicious dinner, Julia. And thanks for inviting me, Red."

"I can get these, Ryan," Hope said, taking the plates from him.

"It's okay, I like to do my part."

Julia got up to join them, but Hope put her hands up. "Oh no. You cooked, the least we can do is clean up."

"Nonsense, I like to help," Julia said, scraping plates.

Ryan looked over at Zach, trying to quietly sneak another brownie, the one he already ate leaving a few crumbs on his lips. "Zach, do you remember that sled you saw at my workshop? How'd you like to go for a sleigh ride some time?"

"Wow, really? Mom promised to take me but she's been really busy."

"I *am* going to take you," Hope said with mock indignation.

"Well, good," he said, "then you can come, too."

"I ... um ... okay," she said, clearly not quite happy about that as she picked up the plate of brownies.

"Awesome," Zach said. "Can I have another brownie?"

"Haven't you already had two?" she said, with a teasing smile.

He nodded begrudgingly. As Hope turned away, Ryan watched Red hand Zach a brownie he'd hidden in his napkin, with a finger to his lips.

"You ladies don't mind if Zach and I get back to work on our project in the garage, do you?" Red asked.

"Oh, go on," Julia said with a chuckle. "You, too, Hope, you've done enough. I hear an attic calling you."

"It's okay, Julia, there's not much left."

Hope put the last of the plates on the counter and Julia began running water at the sink. Suddenly he felt uncomfortable. The dinner was over and everyone had a chore.

"Well, I should get going, too. I'll be back early, Red. Mind if I just leave my tools upstairs?"

"Sure thing. See you tomorrow," Red said before Zach pulled him out of the room.

He drove back home thinking how nice it had been to sit with a family, everyone with something to share. Aside from the military, he'd lived most of his adult life alone. Once, he'd dreamt of something like this. A real home, a family, everything he'd longed for as a kid. Something about Hope was stirring up those feelings again, despite his attempts to push them aside.

He wondered again what had happened to keep Hope away for so long. It was obvious she and her father loved each other. And he could tell she wasn't the type to be unforgiving, not with family.

Whatever had happened years ago, it must have been big.

As Hope turned on the dishwasher, Julia finished wiping

down the counters. She put the sponge in the sink and turned to Hope.

"Your dad's so happy. You know this is the first tree he's put up since you left."

"I'm sure that was more about my mom being gone."

"No, Hope. He made peace with that. There was nothing else he could do, he finally realized that. But with you … "

"Please, Julia, it's been hard for me, too," she said, wiping her hands and turning away to look out the window. "When my mother died, it left a hole in my life, not just my heart. I wasn't even finished with college and my dad made it … let's just say he made it impossible for me to come back afterwards."

Julia put a hand on her arm, and she turned and looked at her.

"You should talk to him, Hope. There's more to this than you know."

"I don't understand. What do you mean?"

Julia turned and began untying her apron. "It's really not my place to say."

Hope walked around the island to face her. "But you know, don't you."

Julia gave her a sad smile. "Don't forget I was your mother's best friend."

"And now my dad's? Or is it more?"

"Oh, Hope, your mom asked me to keep an eye on him when she … " Her eyes filled with tears. "She also asked me to keep an eye on you."

"But I left."

Julia nodded.

"So … what he did back then has something to do with my mom?"

Julia walked over to the other side of the room and picked up her purse and coat. "I'm just saying things aren't always what they seem."

She went out the back door then, leaving Hope to wonder what she could be talking about. But whatever it was, she was clearly uncomfortable sharing it.

It was after eleven when she finally went into her old bed-room, surprised to see Zach standing at the window.

"Zach, you should be asleep by now. What on earth are you doing?"

"I was wondering where the star would be, if there was still a star. It's so dark I can't tell."

She walked to the window, pointing up in the distance. "It is kind of hard to tell now because when it's lit, that's all you see in that whole part of the sky."

"So, when you were in bed and looked out this window, that's all you could see?"

"Yes. But why so many questions?"

Zach shrugged. "I was just wondering." Then he turned and looked up at her. "Mom, are you going to do what all those people were asking? Write about the star?"

"I don't know, Honey."

"Why not?"

"Well, I'm kind of busy, don't you think? I mean there's the attic to pack up still. And now some of the Hometown Holiday.

Plus, we're not even going to be here all that long."

"Well, I could just go to the store with Grandpa every day, so you wouldn't have to worry about me. And Julia said she'll make sure I get all my schoolwork done, remember? I'm actually ahead on that. And Mom?"

"Yes, Honey?"

"Don't you always tell me I can do anything I want if I try hard enough?"

She had to smile. "You have your grandma's heart. Do you know that?"

"So do you. That's what Grandpa said."

"He did?" she asked, trying not to act surprised.

Zach nodded and yawned.

"Okay, my sweet boy, now it really is time for bed."

He climbed into bed and as she kissed his cheek, he whispered, "You should do it, Mom."

"Oh, Honey, we wouldn't even be here to see it lit."

She tucked his blankets around him then turned out the light, ready to head back to the attic for another half hour.

"Mom," Zach said, as she opened the bedroom door. "You could come back when I go with Dad. Then you won't be alone for Christmas."

Sometimes he just undid her. This little nine-year-old boy with a heart as big as that star he wanted. She almost said *we'll see*, but remembered that Zach had already caught on to that. Instead, she said, "That's an idea, Honey. I'll think about it. Now please go to sleep."

As she worked in the attic until after midnight, trying to focus, all she could do was worry. What if Drew bailed on Zach and broke his heart again? What if she didn't find another place to live by the time they had to move? Where would they go? And worst of all, what if she lost her job?

And what on earth did Julia mean when she said there was more to what happened with her father than she knew? Did she even want to go there again?

CHAPTER 6

THEY'D ONLY BEEN HERE A few days, but Hope felt as though she'd already fallen into a rhythm. Zach was at the kitchen counter doing homework, her dad supervising. Before heading into town, she'd put in several hours in the attic, plowing through old clothes and things that should've been thrown out decades ago. The piles of things she'd be taking back south with her were growing, now encompassing half a dozen boxes. An old purse of her mother's. Her warm, fleecy blue robe. She'd already washed it and had been wearing it. How could she have forgotten how cold New Jersey winters could be. And then there was a box of letters and other papers she still couldn't quite bring herself to go through. There was something about seeing her mother's handwriting, her beautiful script, that was particularly painful.

As she kept going through the artifacts of a lifetime, several lifetimes in fact, there was something both beautiful and sad about it. Here were the memories of her parents' lives, her life, and even some from previous generations. Would she ever give that to Zach? Would she ever be able to have the kind of home where they could build real traditions? Where he would have these kinds of memories, as well as the memorabilia to go along with them?

Now, as she walked into town, she thought about the memory that was haunting her. The star. There was no box of artifacts for that. There was simply the absence of it on top of Buck Hill each night. The sadness over that blank space in the sky. She knew her mother would never ... could never ... bear that. She'd have gotten that star up and running the very next Christmas after the storm. Didn't she owe it to her mother, and Zach, to at least look into it?

It was just nine o'clock, the college bells ringing the hour in the distance, and the shops on Main Street were starting to come alive. She turned right past Stella's Café and walked half a block to Wire's Electric. She went inside and the bell rang overhead. An older man looked up from his desk, then stood and came around to her with a big smile.

"Hello, Mr. Durling," she said, smiling back.

"Hi, Hope. Long time no see. Welcome home. I hear you're going to bring our star back."

She sighed, but couldn't help laughing. How did Phoebe manage to tell the entire town what she had not even agreed to?

"That seems to be the word around town, thanks to Phoebe Hodge. Anyway, it's so nice to see you. And actually, that's what I've come to talk to you about, the star. Do you happen to have a few minutes now? Or I could come back later?"

"Sure, now is fine," he said, gesturing toward a table. "You know, my grandfather did the original wiring up there on Buck

Hill, back in the forties when Old Doc Stevens owned the place. Your grandfather helped build it, in fact."

Hope pulled a notebook from her purse. "Yes, I've heard that."

"And when we were boys, your dad and I helped take it down and put it back up each year," he said, the pleasure of his memories evident on his face. "Oh, that was a job, all right. Believe it or not, we used the old wooden poles from the original telegraph lines that once ran along the railroad tracks on Rockport Road."

"Wow, I didn't know that."

"Oh, it was quite a feat. Each year we had to patch and jerry-rig that thing and it took quite a bit of muscle. And my grandfather had to redo a lot of the original wiring each year as well."

"Oh, my gosh, that sounds like a monumental effort to put it up and take it down each year. I had no idea."

"And the weather … well, let's just say it didn't always cooperate. Snow made it tricky, but there were times it would be sleeting. I think your dad caught pneumonia one year."

"What?" She sat there, imagining her father as a boy and then a teenager taking part in the building and taking down of the star year after year. "It's amazing they never missed a year, from what I know."

"Well, back in the sixties somewhere the town had a big fundraiser, and eventually the permanent star went up. That's the one you know."

"That I do remember hearing. And now it's metal."

"That's right. Making it much stronger, of course, until

that crazy superstorm hit it."

Mr. Durling nodded. "We went up, a few of us, right after the storm and … it was a mess. Just getting up there was a nightmare. There were trees down all over town, no power for most for over a week. Worst storm of my life, that's for sure." He shrugged, shaking his head.

"I saw the damage up close. It is pretty bad."

"You know, Hope, there was so much damage to homes and businesses right here in town, and the star would've been a huge project, a lot of money, it just got put on the back burner, and then the property went up for sale. And now … it's hard to believe it hasn't been lit in … it's gotta be seven years."

"Oh … I didn't realize it had been so long."

"I think after all the fixing up here in town, battling with insurance companies, and FEMA, well, people were just exhausted."

"I can imagine. Listen, Mr. Durling, I know it needs a lot of work, I'm not minimizing that. And this might not even be doable. But do you think you could help me get an idea of how much money we'd actually need to try and get it lit again? You were the only one I could think of who might be able to help with this."

He sat back, shaking his head. "Oh, Hope, we're talking about more than just simple electrical work. We'd have to get the power company involved to restore the line, too. Then there's the structural damage to the steel frame and welding to fix it. All of it will take considerable funds."

"Ouch. That sounds like it could be astronomical."

"After that storm, we got estimates on everything but …

people in town were already strapped. And overwhelmed." He ran a hand through his gray hair. "I'm sorry to say, but this might take a miracle."

"Well … I used to believe in them, thanks to our star."

They sat there in silence for a long moment. Then Mr. Durling reached over and put a hand on hers, squeezing. "That star is part of my family's history, Hope, as well as yours. So I'll help you in any way I can."

"You're a sweetheart, Mr. Durling. I can't thank you enough."

"Well, don't thank me yet."

"I know, I know. We're just exploring the possibility, right?" she said, with a little chuckle.

He smiled and nodded. "That's a good way of putting it. Now, let's get an update on the costs and go from there."

She sat at that table for the next hour while Mr. Durling tried to put figures together, going back into his archives for old files on the star, then calling a contact at the power company he'd known for years. By the time she left, her head was spinning. And the amount kept growing until it seemed more impossible than ever. But it was a start.

It was snowing again by the time she began walking back up Main Street toward the Community Center where the Hometown Holiday crew was having another meeting. Many of the shopkeepers were outside, putting up more decorations, fancy wreaths, and all different kinds of lights and small trees flanking their doors. A giant blow-up Grinch stood outside

Marley's Restaurant, even singing his famous song. Everyone called out a "Merry Christmas" and she found herself smiling, despite the growing list of worries in her head.

The Community Center was an old brick three-story building on the far side of Main Street, just next to the historic Presbyterian Church and its old cemetery where she once played. Inside there was a big open room on the first floor where she'd gone to dances in high school, and where they had the Halloween events after that parade. She'd also taken ballet classes here as a little girl, by a dance teacher who came once a week from the city.

She walked in and saw Phoebe, Jane, Norm, Rob and Lori all seated around a big table. The rest of the room was empty, with tables and chairs stacked against the walls. They all turned as she walked in.

"Sorry I'm late, I … " She stopped and looked at their faces. They were all staring at her oddly and she noticed a few eyebrows go up. "What's going on?"

"Nothing," Phoebe said, a little too forcefully, hardly convincing her.

She sat down and Ruth jumped right in. "So, I've got some good news on the Jingle Ball. We've got the band lined up and Grand Rental Station is donating the tent."

"And the Santa Parade now has at least a dozen floats," Norm said with a satisfied smile. "Plus, the high school band and twirlers, and the Colonial Musketeers. So I think we're going to have as good a parade as we've ever had."

"Wow, things are really coming along," Hope said, surprised at the sudden progress. "I've got ten stores committed to the ice sculpture contest now. And Jane, how about the horse and carriages?"

"All set. Donaldson Farms is donating everything, including the drivers."

"Great work," she said. "Now let's pray nothing falls apart at the last minute."

"Like another superstorm," Norm said.

Phoebe cleared her throat suddenly, and as if it were a signal, everyone else was now shuffling papers that seemed to require some fierce attention.

"Okay, what's going on?" she asked, turning right to Phoebe.

"You haven't heard WRNJ this morning?" Phoebe asked her.

Slowly she shook her head. "No ... why?" She looked around the table at the faces that were avoiding her and glancing guiltily at each other.

Now Norm cleared his throat loudly. "Well, I kind of mentioned ... on air that is ... that you might be writing an ... oh an inspirational piece for a star fund and, well, people have already started calling in with donations."

"Wait ... what?" Now it all made sense. How everyone she'd talked to that morning knew. They must've heard on the radio earlier. But still, this was Phoebe's doing. And her friend had the good grace now to at least look sheepish.

"Well, I might've mentioned it to a few people and ... it kind of ... well, it's taken on a life of its own. And Hope, everyone got so excited that there might even be a chance to get our star back, and everyone agreed you're the person to do this. So ... what do you say?"

She sat there, annoyed, terrified, overwhelmed, yet thinking of Zach climbing all the way up Buck Hill their first morning here. And then last night in bed, urging her to do this. She'd given him so little. And of course, there was her mother's legacy.

"I can't believe you did this," she said to Phoebe, "but I say yes!"

They all jumped up, clapping and cheering and hugging each other, and then her. Each of them whispered encouragement in her ear, and gratitude.

Phoebe was last to hug her. "Thanks for making me sweat it out."

"I kind of decided last night. You know my mother would never have given up on it, she'd have done it for me. And now ... I'm doing it for Zach. And maybe a wee bit for myself. And you," she said with a teasing smile."

"People are already donating!" Phoebe said.

Jane came over then. "And Hope, there really isn't a ton of time. I'm going to need your article by this Sunday night at the very latest to get it in next week's *Gazette*."

"But this is Wednesday."

"Right. You've got four days to write it," Phoebe said. "You can do it. And that'll give us roughly another week to raise the money and then a week to get the work done for Christmas Eve. It's doable."

She sighed, her brief euphoria deflating suddenly. "I went to see Mr. Durling this morning about all of the electrical repairs along with the structural work needed and ... we're going to need a lot of money. This is way more than I could have imagined. And what if … what if we do all this, and get everyone's hopes up, and it doesn't happen?"

"We have to at least try," Phoebe pleaded. "We can't not try."

"It's going to take a miracle," Jane agreed.

"Yes, Mr. Durling said the same thing."

And now it all depended on her. "Oh my gosh … what have I gotten myself into. This is going to be a pressure cooker. Not to mention everything else I have to get done while I'm here."

As the doubts piled up, the rest of the crew began to head out, leaving just her and Phoebe.

"I know this is a lot to ask, Hope. I really do," Phoebe said, giving her a serious look. "But I'm so happy you're doing this."

"Like I really had a choice."

"Come on, you know no one can write this like you. Besides, the star is in your blood."

"I know, but honestly I'm terrified of not living up to everyone's expectations. Especially Zach's. And the timeline is insane! So is the amount of money we'll need."

Phoebe took both her hands and squeezed. "Hope, everyone wants the star back. And it's Christmas. It's the perfect time to do it."

"Well … not exactly perfect for me."

"Hey, I seem to remember a girl I once knew who always said she worked best under pressure. Studying for finals at the last minute. Deciding to sew your own prom gown a week before the dance. And how about pulling an all-nighter to write that graduation speech."

"I was a lot younger then, remember. My life a heck of a lot simpler. And my plate wasn't overflowing like it is now."

"I know," Phoebe said softly, her eyes filling with tears. "I get it. I do. And I want you to know how much I appreciate this. And so will everyone in this town who's missed the star."

Phoebe hugged her goodbye and left. She sat down again, alone in the big room, scared, yet excited. All she could think about was Zach last night, repeating her own words back to her. *You can do anything you want if you try hard enough.* Those were actually her own mother's words to her each and every time she doubted herself when she was young. And her mother had been right. But this was different. It wasn't just her. It was an entire town full of people she needed to appeal to so that they would open their wallets—right before Christmas when so many were already strapped. And after so many had spent years, apparently, putting their homes and businesses back on track after that superstorm.

There was so much not in her control. All she had, really, was her writing. She needed to write the best article she possibly could. But even if she tried her very best, would it still be enough?

By the time she walked up her father's driveway, Hope's mind was racing with ideas for the star article. Her thoughts were suddenly interrupted by laughter and she stopped, looking over at the garage to see Ryan and Zach coming out the side door.

"Hey, guys, what's going on?" she said coming closer.

Zach ran and stopped her in her tracks. "Mom! I told you! You can't go in the garage anymore."

Ryan gave her a wink and raised a hand, zipping his lip. Zach gave him a high five.

"Okay, okay, I get it. I promise I won't venture near it again. Now, where's my dad? I need to talk to him."

"He had some problem back at the store," Ryan said, "so Zach and I ... are helping him with some stuff in the garage."

"Oh," she said, disappointed. "I guess it'll have to wait."

"Mom, can we go sleigh riding tomorrow? Please, please?" Zach asked with that pleading look.

She hesitated, wondering how to fit that in with everything else. Ryan and Zach were both looking at her.

"Ummm ... . sure. I guess if it's okay with Ryan."

He nodded. "Works for me."

"Awesome!" Zach exclaimed, then took Ryan by the hand and led him back into the garage.

Hope just stood there watching, amazed once again at the transformation in her son since they arrived just a few days ago. Maybe she shouldn't feel so guilty about not spending much time with him. Between her dad and Ryan, they seemed to be giving him more than enough. And he was obviously loving it.

Ryan looked up from his workbench, wondering who could be knocking on his door at this hour. It was nearly nine. He wasn't expecting anyone.

"Come in," he called out.

The door didn't open. Kodi had already gone to the door

but wasn't barking, so it had to be someone he knew. He put his drill down and went over and opened the door. There stood Lauren, smiling and holding a round chocolate cake in both hands.

"Happy Birthday!" she cried. "Sorry, I couldn't get the door! I hope you like chocolate."

He stood there, stunned. Before he could say a word, she marched in, setting the cake on the big work table and putting down her purse.

"I do like chocolate, but ... how on earth did you know it's my birthday?"

She turned to him and slipped off her coat. She was wearing a black dress with a plunging neckline. He hoped she'd come from a date or something and hadn't dressed like that for him.

"I remembered it from your application you submitted to do the repairs to the Christmas decorations," she said, with a satisfied grin.

"Listen, Lauren, you really shouldn't have."

"Yes, I should have! Everyone's birthday should be celebrated. And I figured you were probably doing nothing at all about it. Am I right?"

"Well, right," he said and couldn't help smiling.

"Okay, then," she said, turning and pulling paper plates and a knife out of her big purse and setting them on the table.

"Wow, you don't fool around," he said, a bit stunned by it all.

"Oh, you have no idea," she said, giving him a suggestive look. "Now, I did forget matches."

"Oh, no, no candles, no singing, none of that."

"No singing, one candle. Deal?"

He sighed. "Okay, deal. There's a lighter right there by my toolbox. Let me clean my hands off."

He went to the back of the workshop where he had rags and hand sanitizer. He poured sanitizer into his palms and rubbed it in, then wiped it off and turned around.

"Okay, I—" he began to say, but Lauren clicked the lighter, and a second later, a sparkler burst into flame, flashing and throwing off sparks on top of the cake, and his lungs seized. He couldn't take a breath, it burned. Then his legs went weak.

"Happy birthday—"

"Stop! Stop it!"

"I'm sorry! Ryan, what is it?"

He turned away, closing his eyes but not before he could see the disappointment on her face. But in that moment, he wasn't there in his workshop. He was somewhere else entirely.

He wasn't sure how much time passed, but when he turned, Lauren had packed everything and was standing there with her coat buttoned up. Her eyes shone with unshed tears.

"I'm sorry," he said, walking over to her. "It's nothing you did, I'm just ... I'm not used to a fuss."

She looked at him hesitantly.

"Did you make the cake?" he asked, forcing a small smile to try to change the mood.

She nodded. "Chocolate fudge cake and chocolate icing. The kind my mom always made for me."

"I do like chocolate. If it isn't too late, that is."

"Sure," she said, taking her coat off again.

The cake was delicious and after a few bites, Lauren began talking a blue streak as she usually did. He knew she was interested in him as more than a friend and he didn't want to encourage that. But she also seemed lonely, and he saw her often rub people the wrong way and felt sorry for her. Still, he had to be careful. It was a fine line with her, being friendly without giving her the wrong idea.

CHAPTER 7

THE NEXT AFTERNOON, HOPE AND Ryan headed up a snowy trail on the side of Buck Hill with Zach ahead of them pulling the old refurbished sled.

"Thanks for doing this," she said to Ryan. "I haven't seen Zach this excited in a long time."

"You're welcome."

"I feel like I've been neglecting him since I got here."

"Oh, I think he's having a good time with your dad. I wouldn't worry."

"I know. My dad's been great with him. I've been wanting to talk to my dad alone, though. But if he's not with Zach, he's at the store."

Ryan stopped and turned to her. "Is everything okay?"

She stopped, too, nodding. "I just need to ask him about something. We've had a ... rift since my mom died. My dad can be so stubborn."

Ryan gave a little laugh. "I think maybe you inherited that from your dad."

She smiled. "Maybe. My mom was always the peacemaker."

"Your dad's a great guy, Hope. You're lucky to have him."

"I know that."

"But?"

"But ... it's complicated."

"Right. So you've said."

She began walking again and he followed. She'd forgotten how quiet and peaceful the woods could be in the winter. Up ahead, Zach was pulling the sled and whistling, something he'd picked up from her dad.

"So how did it go with the merchants and the ice sculptures yesterday?" Ryan asked, breaking her thoughts.

"Oh, that was a bit of a challenge," she laughed. "Every single one of them was more determined to tell me a story about the star and how it impacted their lives. I mean, it wasn't the point of my visit, but I have to say ... there were some amazing stories."

"I heard on WRNJ that you're writing an article to help raise money to rebuild the star."

She stopped again and turned to him. "I actually ... am. Yes."

Ryan shook his head. "That would take a miracle, Hope. You saw the star, how much work it needs. You're not talking about some quick, cheap fix. It's going to—"

"So I keep hearing," she cut him off. "But don't you believe in miracles, Ryan?"

He looked away and she wondered if he was counting to ten, his annoyance no longer veiled. "I can't say that I do," he finally said.

"You know, I stopped believing in them, too, a while back.

But hearing the stories of all these people again, the longing and the love … I'm starting to believe in them again."

Ryan sighed. "Look, I may not be into Christmas, but do you have any real idea how much money this will take? The wiring alone—"

"I've been doing my homework, so yes, I do."

"Hope, even if I agreed, there would never be enough time for me to get it done with everything—"

"What!? Ryan, no one is asking you to do the work!"

"You're not getting it. I build and fix things. And it's my home. Do you think I'm going to let someone else up on my property and watch them fix it?"

"Why not? I mean this is way more than a one-person job!"

He just stood there, shaking his head.

"Ryan, if we somehow make this miracle happen, if we raise enough money, are you going to stand in our way?"

Still, he just stood there, hands on his hips, staring into the woods.

"There's been a star shining over Hackettstown at Christmas ever since the soldiers came home from World War II. Can you imagine that? The miracle of seeing the star as they came home from foreign lands? Wondering if they were even going to make it back? It's been a symbol of home for everyone who lives here for generations. And a symbol of hope. If we somehow manage to do this, you won't be able to—"

"Hurry up, slowpokes!" Zach's voice yelled from above. "You're taking too long! I'm at the top!"

"Almost there," she called back, then turned to Ryan once again.

"I won't be able to what?" he asked, clearly annoyed now.

She sighed, not wanting to ruin this for Zach. "Look, why don't we talk about this another time. Let's just have fun with Zach, okay? He's really been looking forward to it."

Ryan hesitated, then nodded, walking on. She followed and a few minutes later, they reached the top of the trail where Zach was jumping up and down, Kodi at his side, tail wagging. Ryan took a treat from his pocket.

"Can I give it to him?" Zach asked.

Ryan went over and handed the treat to Zach. "Now make him sit and then hold it out like this, with your palm up."

Zach followed the instructions. Kodi inhaled the treat, then licked Zach's hand. "I think he likes me," Zach said, giggling as Kodi kept licking.

"I think you're right. Now, are you ready for your first sleigh ride?"

"Ready!"

Ryan pulled the sled to the top of the run and pushed it down a bit into the snow, then sat on it to the rear. "Okay, Zach, you hop on in front of me. Once you get the hang of it, you can try it by yourself, okay?"

"Okay!"

Zach sat in front of Ryan, who put an arm around him then pushed off with his other hand. They began to move slowly, then with one more push, they suddenly took off. She could hear Zach laughing, his voice fading the farther down the hill they went. Beside her, Kodi whined a little, no doubt wondering if they were coming back. But within minutes Zach was racing back up to the top where she and Kodi waited, cheeks flushed, hat askew, smiling ear to ear.

"Mom, that was so fun! You have to try it!"

"Oh no. I've done my fair share of sledding when I was younger, you keep going."

"Ryan will steer, Mom."

"Well, you know that's a lot faster than I remember … "

Suddenly Ryan appeared again. "You're not chicken, are you, Hope?" he said with a teasing smile.

"Ha! Not on your life!" She was actually scared but wasn't about to give him the satisfaction. She walked over to the sled and looked him straight in the eye. "Let's go."

He gave her a gallant wave and she sat on the sled, pulling her knees to her chest. Ryan sat behind her then, his legs and arms suddenly wrapped around her and pulling her so close, she could feel his warmth and caught the faint smell of a spicy cologne. She glanced behind her. Ryan's blue eyes were locked on hers for a long moment, but there was no teasing look any longer. For a second it felt as if her heart stopped.

"Ready, set, go!" Zach yelled.

Ryan broke the look, released one hand and gave them a shove. A moment later they were flying down the hill and she was laughing out loud, then screaming when they hit a bump at the bottom and tumbled off as the sled turned sideways. She landed on her back and lay there, catching her breath. She looked over to see Ryan just a few feet away on his back, watching her.

"Oh my gosh, I forgot how much fun that is," she laughed.

Ryan said nothing, then reached over and gently brushed snow off her cheek. She stared at him and his eyes seemed to be searching hers.

"Hurry up!" Zach yelled from up top. "It's my turn again."

Ryan jumped up suddenly and offered her a hand, helping her up. They each brushed snow off themselves and she began walking quickly, her face hot, though she wondered if it might be from the look and not the exertion. They walked back to the top without saying a word.

The sky was already darkening when they arrived back in Ryan's driveway. Hope was exhausted, but she could see Zach was still full of excitement despite all the exercise. Ryan, she noticed, was limping a bit more.

"Either of you hungry?" he asked as they got to her car. "I'm making pizza tonight."

"Pizza! I'm starving!"

"Zach, we've taken so much of Ryan's time already."

Ryan smiled at Zach. "It's fine. It'll be nice to have the company. It's usually just me and Kodi. And Kodi, well, he's not much of a talker."

Zach giggled at that. At the sound of his name, Kodi began wagging his tail excitedly. Zach began petting him.

"Okay, but only if we can help, right Zach?"

Zach nodded.

"Deal," Ryan said, and led them to his house, an A-frame just past the workshop. They walked inside a 2-story great room with a loft above. It was rustic, with wood beams and a soaring stone fireplace. Ryan went right over and lit a fire that had already been laid. Zach went over and watched as she hung up their coats on hooks in the hall.

"Where's your Christmas tree?" Zach asked Ryan as she walked closer to warm her hands.

"I don't have one," Ryan said, stuffing more newspaper under the logs.

"How come?"

"Zach," she cautioned. "That's personal."

"It's okay, Hope. Well, Zach, I'm working a lot and since I was in the Marines, I kind of got used to not having one. We'd usually have a big one on the base, so … I never really got in the habit."

"Don't you miss having one?" Zach asked with a frown.

Ryan smiled, shaking his head. "I get all the Christmas I need down in town. Now, how about a root beer?"

"Sure."

"Hope, would you like a glass of wine."

"I'd love one. Now what can we do to help?"

They followed Ryan to the other side of the great room to an open kitchen with a large center island. Ryan opened the fridge and took out the soda and a bottle of wine, setting them on the island.

"How about I'll roll out the dough? Zach, you can grate the mozzarella cheese. And Hope, you can cut the veggies."

"Sounds good."

As darkness fell, the house took on a cozy atmosphere with the fire crackling and the inside warming from the oven and hearth. Zach entertained them with riddles, stumping Ryan over and over.

"Ryan, what starts with a P, ends with an E, and has thousands of letters?"

Ryan smiled, looking dramatically puzzled as he rolled out the dough. "I have no idea, Zach. What?"

"The post office!"

"Hah, that's a good one."

"Okay, this one's easy," Zach said, already laughing. "What do you have that your friends use more?"

Hope watched Ryan shaking his head, giving Zach more puzzled looks, then finally shrugging his shoulders.

"I give up, Zach."

"Your name!" he laughed. "That was an easy one!"

"Definitely not an easy one," Ryan said, as he finished stretching the dough and laid it in the pizza pan. "Okay now, do you want to put the sauce and cheese on?"

"Sure."

Zach carefully ladled the sauce on, then sprinkled the cheese.

"Now how about the veggies?"

"Do I have to have vegetables?" he groaned.

"No, it's okay," Hope said with a smile.

"So, we'll do one plain and one veggie," Ryan said, sliding the cut vegetables over to Zach. "How about you decorate the veggie pie."

She and Ryan watched, smiling, as Zach created a crazy face with the veggie pie, complete with hair, eyebrows, nose and a big smile made out of red pepper strips. Finally, Ryan slid the pies into the oven. All the while Kodi never left Zach's side. Hope watched as she set the island with plates and utensils. More riddles followed until ten minutes later when the timer went off.

"Pizza's ready," Ryan said, pulling the pies out and placing them on the counter. He sliced them expertly and slid pieces onto their plates. Hope was already feeling so relaxed she had to stifle a few yawns, between the exercise and cold, then coming into the warm house, and now the wine.

"So, what do you think?" Ryan asked Zach after his first bite.

"Awesome!" he said. "I never made pizza before."

Ryan glanced at her.

"Guilty," she admitted. "I usually get it delivered on Friday nights because I'm too tired from working all week."

"This is way better, Mom."

"Okay, okay, I can't argue with that."

Zach polished off two slices with gusto and suddenly yawned. Ryan stood and took his plate.

"You look tired, Honey," she said, gathering the other plates.

"Do I have to clean up?"

Ryan laughed. "Why don't you hit the couch. I'm sure Kodi will keep you company. The TV remote is on the end table."

"Thanks, Ryan. Is that okay, Mom?"

"Sure thing, Zach."

As she and Ryan carried everything to the sink, back and forth, she could see his limp worsen again.

"Is your leg bothering you?"

He stopped and looked at her, then shrugged. "Sometimes after a long day it does. Or if it's raining. Or snowing." He gave a little laugh.

"I'm sorry if we wore you out."

"No, no, not at all. This was a nice day. Really."

"Can I ask … how it happened?"

Ryan hesitated.

"I'm sorry, I shouldn't have—"

He put a hand up, stopping her. Then he sat back again on a stool and she did, too. He took a sip of his wine and she could see him gathering his thoughts.

"I was in Iraq. I had just signed up for another tour. Our squad was on its way back from a mission, just the four of us." He paused and she could see that he seemed far away, as if he were seeing it all again. "We probably should have paid more attention to our surroundings. We always did, of course, but this day we were anxious to get back to the base because … they were having a little Christmas party and … there was going to be great food, and beer, and lots of homemade cookies sent from home. It was just one lax moment really, but … anyway there was a massive IED and … I was the only one who came home."

She was picturing it all, and Ryan in the midst of it. He was staring into his glass of wine. She reached over and put a hand on his arm. "Oh, Ryan, I am so very sorry. I can't even imagine."

He shook his head suddenly as if coming back to the present. "This limp, the pain, it's nothing compared to … " he shrugged.

"I understand now … why you're not really into Christmas. I'm sorry if I gave you a hard time about that."

"It's not just that. Growing up in foster care, let's just say I don't have the memories that you do."

"I'm sorry." She tried to picture him, a little boy, then a teenager, never having a real home, or a real Christmas. "You know, it's not too late to make memories. I hope you'll come to all of the Hometown Holiday festivities. You'll see how special it is. Besides, you're actually a part of it now, you know. You're helping to make it happen."

"I thought you weren't staying for all of it?"

"Well, things just keep getting more complicated and I have to be here for—"

Her cell phone rang just then and she pulled it out of her purse. "Sorry, it's my dad."

"Hey Dad ... Oh, Julia. What? Oh, I ... I'll be there as quickly as I can. Yes, okay. Thank you."

She stood and looked at Ryan, suddenly trembling all over. "My dad just got rushed to the hospital. I have to go."

He was already going for their coats. "I'll drive you. You shouldn't be driving upset like this."

"Let's drop Zach off, please. Julia said she'll watch him. I don't want him to worry."

They both looked over to see Zach asleep on the couch, with Kodi sleeping beside him. They pulled on their coats and she slid Zach's on him as Ryan lifted him from the couch.

As they drove to the hospital after dropping off Zach, who barely woke up and went straight to bed, Hope's mind raced. It was like a video trailer of a movie, and her dad was in every scene. She was a little girl, riding piggyback on his shoulders as he cut the grass in the yard, feeling like the queen of the world up there. Then she was coming down the stairs in her prom gown, her dad all teary-eyed and trying to hide it with his stern scowl, as if he didn't approve of her dress. And then that final time she left, a year after her mom died when she graduated college, longing to get as far away from her pain, and her father, as possible. And now ...

She felt her hand squeezed and looked over to Ryan, who was giving her an assuring smile as he drove. And then they were in the ER parking lot, and he grabbed the first spot he could find. She jumped out before the truck had barely stopped.

Ryan was right behind her as the glass doors slid open and she raced to the receptionist.

"I'm here for Red, I mean Charles McClain. I'm his daughter."

The receptionist looked down at her desk and then picked up her phone. "Charles McClain's daughter is here." She paused, then hung up. "They're just finishing up a test."

"Is he okay?"

"Doctor said he's stable. Why don't you have a seat and I'll call you as soon as they'll let you in."

Ryan took her hand and led her to the seating area but she couldn't sit. Somehow this felt like a dream. This wasn't happening. What if ...

"I need to talk to him," she said as she paced.

Ryan stopped her. "Hey, it sounds like he's okay. Don't panic."

"But ... I never should have stayed away so long, I need to ... " Her voice cracked and then hot tears slid down her cheeks. "I was so angry at him."

"Hope," Ryan said softly, tilting her face to look at him, "we all do things we regret. It's not too late."

"I hope so."

His blue eyes were so full of compassion. Gently he wiped her tears, as they stared at each other, his fingers so soft as they touched her face. Whispering it would all be okay. And then he was coming closer, and she felt herself lifting her face as his lips reached toward hers—

"Miss McClain, you can go back now."

Quickly she pulled away, turning, her face flaming.

"I'll wait here," she heard Ryan say behind her.

The receptionist ushered her back into the Emergency area to a small cubicle. When she pulled the curtain aside, there was her father sitting on a hospital bed. Red McClain, who'd always been this big, larger-than-life force of nature, suddenly looked so fragile in a hospital gown, hooked up to a machine. Beside him, a middle-aged woman in a white jacket was writing on a chart.

"Hope," her dad said, as he noticed her.

"Dad, are you okay?"

"Your father is fine," the woman said, turning to her. "I'm Dr. Barrett, staff cardiologist here."

"What happened, Dr. Barrett?"

"I was just telling your father that he needs to slow down. His heart's strong, but his blood pressure is elevated. He's got some tachycardia, and that's all no doubt where the dizziness came from. Overwork and stress at his age are not a good combination."

Her father was shaking his head. "I wasn't overdoing it,

there's just a lot going on right now and—"

"Don't worry, Dr. Barrett," she said, cutting her father off. "I'll make sure he slows down."

Dr. Barrett nodded, then looked at her dad again. "The nurse will bring his discharge papers and a prescription for that blood pressure. I want him to follow up in a week for a nuclear stress test and a monitor he'll wear for two weeks. He may need a beta-blocker for the heart rhythm."

"Consider it done," she said as her father glared at her. "And thank you so much."

Dr. Barrett took her chart and left and her father began to get up.

"Dad, wait! Before we go, I need to talk—"

"We can talk at home, Hope."

"Dad, please, this can't wait."

He paused, seated on the edge of the hospital bed. "What is it?"

She took a deep breath. "I need to ask you something, Dad. After Mom died, before I left, what … happened?"

"What do you mean?"

"Julia told me that things aren't as they seemed."

Her father's eyes narrowed and his face turned red. He stood up suddenly, clearly upset.

"She shouldn't have—"

"Dad, please! We need to finally—"

"Hope, there's nothing to discuss! Now step outside, I need to get out of this ridiculous hospital gown."

She let out a long, frustrated sigh, then turned and waited outside the cubicle.

Red McClain tried to keep calm as he got dressed. The last thing he wanted to do was get lightheaded again and end up being admitted overnight, something Dr. Barrett had warned could happen when he first arrived.

He tried not to show how nervous he was when he walked into the ER, out of breath and dizzy. It was panic, he kept telling himself, not his heart. But now he knew it wasn't that simple. Things in his body weren't working the way they should be. He was seventy-two years old and he was scared. And he didn't want to die. Not when Hope was back in his life. And Zach. He could see how much Zach needed a father figure around. He loved that little boy so much it almost hurt.

He would listen and do whatever the doctor said. He wanted to be around to see his grandson grow up. To see the man he would become. He hoped to be part of their lives again. Something Alice would never have. It broke his heart just imagining the joy she would have found in her grandchild. Each time Zach made his heart light up, he kept thinking: *You should be here to see this.* It seemed so unfair that she missed so much. But life wasn't fair, he knew that all too well now.

Thinking of Alice brought him right back to the problem at hand. Julia should never have said anything to Hope. There was no need to. Yes, there was past damage, and yes, his relationship with his daughter had suffered tremendously, but now … now things were turning out better than he could have imagined. Zach was a wonder, so bright and so excited by their project. They were bonding in a way he couldn't have imagined a few weeks ago.

His hands shook as he buttoned his flannel shirt, warning himself that he might be jumping the gun in worrying. He would try to ignore Hope's questions. Besides, she was so busy, she might just forget all about it. After all, why open up something that happened years ago? Something he promised himself would never happen. He had to protect Alice.

As he pulled on his jacket and zipped it up, he whispered to himself, "What have you done, Julia?"

CHAPTER 8

HOPE WALKED INTO THE KITCHEN to find Zach and her dad eating lunch. She put a stack of games and puzzles on the center island counter where they sat.

"I found these in the attic, Zach. These are some classic games I think you'll love, like Clue. Grandpa was always pretty good at it, right Dad? Because you're going to stay home from work one more day and take it easy."

Her father rolled his eyes. "Come on, Honey, I stayed home yesterday. I've got work and … " he glanced at Zach, "a project to finish."

"Well, let's just take your blood pressure one more time before I go." She reached for the BP monitor she bought on the way home from the ER two nights ago and slid the cuff on her father's arm, pumping as he muttered under his breath. She watched the numbers as the gauge began moving down. "You're still a smidge over normal."

"That's because you're—" he started to say in an irate tone, then paused, taking a deep breath to calm himself. "Okay, okay, one more day."

"Also, I scheduled those tests for you, the stress test and echo-cardiogram. They're on your calendar, first week of January."

He got up then and gave her a hug, surprising her. "Thank you, Honey. I appreciate your concern."

"Of course, Dad." She smiled and then turned to her son. "Zach, I think there's enough here to keep you both entertained, okay?"

"Sure, Mom. I think Grandpa might like these better than my video games," he said, giggling.

Her dad nodded. "Nothing like a good old-fashioned board game. How about Monopoly, Zach?"

"Oh, good. That ought to take the rest of the afternoon." Hope picked up her tote bag. "By the way, Dad, I'm surprised we haven't seen Julia in a few days."

"Oh, I'm sure she's busy with Christmas shopping," he answered without looking at her.

Hope frowned, recalling her father's whispered words to himself that she overheard at the ER as she waited outside his cubicle. *What have you done, Julia?* She had a feeling something was going on with them now. But it would have to wait until later. She slipped on her coat.

"Where are you off to?" her dad asked.

"Oh, I just need a break from writing. Walking usually helps me when I'm stuck."

She'd just gotten into the foyer when she heard her son.

"Don't be mad we can't work on the float, Grandpa. Mom just worries a lot."

"I know, Zach. I'm not mad. That means she cares and that's a good thing. I just want to get it finished in time."

"I have an idea. Maybe we can ask Ryan to help us finish it?"

"Now why didn't I think of that?" her father said.

Then she heard a hand slap and realized they'd high-fived. She closed the front door softly, with a smile. Those two were becoming quite a team.

As she walked down Main Street, Hope's mind was swimming with everything she needed to accomplish in the next few days. She was getting down to the wire. Of course, the last day and a half keeping her dad quiet, and well-fed with healthy foods, scheduling his appointments and dealing with his insurance companies so he wouldn't stress ... that had cost her precious time. And time was quickly running short. She was just crossing Grand Avenue, lost in thought when her cell phone rang. Pulling it out of her purse, she smiled.

"Lily! Hi!"

"Well, I can't believe you've been gone a week already," Lily said in her classic Southern drawl. "How goes it in Christmas Town?"

"Haha, it's Hackettstown. But the pressure is on, I've got the rest of today and tomorrow to get the Christmas Star article done."

"For the *Tribune?*"

"No for the *Gazette* here in town."

"Wait, are you serious? You're writing an article for the newspaper up there? This is in addition to the Hometown Holiday you told me about the other day? And your article for the *Tribune* to save your job?"

She paused. When Lily put it like that, it did sound a bit crazy. "Well ... yes."

"That's insane!" Lily said, echoing her thoughts. "And ... wait, are you still packing up your dad's attic?"

"Uh ... yes. But that's kind of on the back burner right now. People are already sending in donations for the star and the editor is going to print an early edition of the *Gazette*, plus get it online as soon as I send it to her. Then it'll get blasted all over social media and on WRNJ, our local station. Hopefully, we can inspire more people to give. I'm hoping to get the star lit again by Christmas Eve."

There was a long silence on Lily's end. Finally, she said, "Honey, are you sure you know what you're doing?"

She gave a little laugh that held little humor. "Oh, I've always worked best under pressure."

"But what about your *Tribune* article that you were so worried about when you left here? How's that going?"

"I still ... can't decide on an approach. 'Christmas in the City' turns out to be much harder to write about than Christmas in a charming small town. Especially with our star."

"When is the *Tribune* article due?"

"Ummm ... the same time."

"Oh, Honey, I hope you know what you're doing."

She could just see Lily shaking her head, her soft blonde curls bouncing.

"Lil, I can't not do this. For a lot of reasons."

"So ... " Lily went on, "how much longer are you staying? And what about Zach and school?"

"Actually, I'm so lucky there. My mom's old friend, Julia, who lives next door, is a retired teacher and has been helping Zach with his schoolwork and even coordinating with his teacher and he's doing great. So, we'll be here a little bit longer than I originally thought."

"But you'll be back here for Drew to take Zach?"

"Of course, though he's been waffling now. He actually called me the other day to suggest I let Zach fly to California to meet him and his latest girlfriend, Marisa. I said no way."

"Good for you."

"There's something going on there. I just can't put my finger on it. But I'm not letting him disappoint Zach again."

"What do you think could be going on?"

"You know, he seems actually serious about this girl-friend. And Hawaii is an unusual place to take your kid for Christmas. I'm just praying he's not planning something like a … surprise wedding."

"Oh my … you can't be serious."

"Drew loves the grand gestures. He sure wooed me with them. Until I realized … oh never mind, I'm just praying it's nothing like that. That would be awful for Zach who's imagining a great vacation and time with his dad, only to have it be more about his dad wooing and impressing Marisa."

"Well, good luck, Hope, and please keep me posted. You know I'm here for you, anything you need."

"What I really need is for you to find me another place to live, Lil. Soon. One that'll keep Zach in the same school, and near all his friends."

"And me! I know, Hope. Believe me, I'm working on it."

Hope stopped walking. She was in front of Wire's Electric now. "I have to go now, Lil. I'm hoping to get the final estimate on the star."

"Okay, but let me know how it all turns out."

"Will do."

"Good luck!"

She hung up, then opened the door and walked into Wire's, hoping Mr. Durling wasn't about to blow her hopes out of the water.

While Hope was gone, Red and Zach quickly donned their coats and went out to the garage to continue working on their float. Red had called Ryan, who was now there, as well. He assured them both he was simply going to watch. No one wanted to get in trouble with Hope.

Now Red stood beside his flatbed truck, which was slowly transforming into the scene that Zach had envisioned. Ryan and Zach were on the truck bed, with Zach helping Ryan measure a vertical board, which would become a wall.

"Okay, we can easily cut a window out of the board right here," Ryan explained, using his hand to outline where the window would go. Zach nodded enthusiastically.

"Great. And I've got an old window in the back there we can maybe fit in if you want to take a look at it," said Red.

"A real window! Cool," Zach said.

Ryan jumped off the truck, with Zach following, and together they measured the window. "We'll make it fit. What do you think, Zach?"

"I think it's gonna be awesome!"

Red was touched at how much Ryan was letting Zach help. Obviously, they could have been much further along if he hadn't. But the change in Zach from when he first walked in the door days ago, a shy and worried little boy, he marveled at it once again. Even Hope was becoming more like her old self, despite everything she'd taken on. She'd been wound so tight when she first arrived, and he knew she was being protective of her son. And herself.

Too many years had gone by since things had fallen apart between them and at first, he thought there was no chance of rectifying things. But now that she'd gotten involved in the Christmas festivities, he could see that light begin to shine again in her eyes. Each night he got in bed and whispered to Alice in the dark, as he always did. But now it was different. *Our girl is back, my love. And our grandson is a treasure. You would be over the moon for him. And I'll make sure nothing ever gets in the way again, I promise.*

Best of all, she hadn't mentioned Julia's comments again. Hopefully, it was all over.

"Red?"

Suddenly Red was back in the moment and Zach and Ryan were staring at him. "Sorry, I was just imagining our finished float."

"We still have to make the star, Grandpa," Zach said so seriously.

Ryan nodded. "I'll need some special tools for that. Maybe you can come up to my workshop tomorrow, Zach, and help me make one. Okay?"

"Cool!" Zach said with a fist bump.

"I'd be happy to bring him up, Ryan," Red said, smiling. "Now, we'd better get a move on before your mom gets back, Zach."

The sun was setting when Hope walked back from Wire's and finally headed up her dad's driveway. She hesitated at the closed garage door, listening. She could hear them talking inside. She knocked loudly. "What's going on in there? Dad, are you doing something foolish?"

A moment later, Ryan came out the side door and closed it fast. He was smiling.

"Did I hear my dad's voice in there? He's not supposed to be working."

"He's not, Hope. He's just ... supervising. Don't worry. I've got this."

She sighed. "Thanks, I really appreciate it."

"He's a good dad. And a wonderful grandfather."

"I know. Zach seems to love being with him. And my dad ... " she shook her head.

"I've known your dad for a while now. This is ... " he shrugged.

"What?"

"Look, I know you've got some guilt issues going on with your dad and I don't want to add to it. But I've never seen him happier."

"Well, thanks, but that does add on to the pile. It's not just guilt, though, it's ... " Now she shrugged. What was it really? So much time had gone by. Patterns had been established. Was there really no hope for them? But there was something that was missing in what she knew. She was certain of that now. And her father was going to keep dodging her, that was obvious. And she couldn't upset him, not now after the heart scare.

"Whatever it is, he's a good guy, Hope. And you're a good woman and a wonderful mother."

The way he said it, the way his eyes warmed looking at her, she couldn't help but remember how close they had come to kissing at the ER. It would have been a mistake, she knew that, but she'd wanted it. And she'd been thinking about it ever since. Now she felt her face beginning to redden.

"Oh, it looks like Julia's home," she said suddenly, nodding to the car that pulled into the driveway next door. "I've been trying to find a moment to talk to her alone. Thanks again for being so good to Zach, and my dad."

"Anytime. And listen, there's an open mic tonight at Mama's. Phoebe and some of the others are coming … if you'd like to come, too."

"Oh? I … "

He flushed. "It's no big deal. I know you're busy and—"

"No, I'd like to," she said, without thinking. "I think you're the one who asked what I ever do for fun so … yes. Sometimes letting my mind relax helps my writing."

"Good. Okay then."

Neither one of them moved, or broke the look.

And then the side garage door opened and Zach yelled out, "Ryan, we need you!"

They both laughed and he turned with a nod. She walked back down the driveway toward Julia's house

Julia's house was smaller than her dad's next door, a charming yellow ranch with window boxes now filled with holly and twinkling lights, a small porch draped in pine garland, and one of her gorgeous, handmade wreaths decorated with red berries and bright cardinals on the front door.

As Hope stepped onto Julia's porch, two decades of memories flitted by, and once again she was seeing herself at various ages running in or out of this same door. How many times had she run here after school to fetch her mother? Best friends since childhood, her mom and Julia were more like sisters. Julia had been her mom's college roommate, as well as her maid of honor. Their afternoon teas were legendary and when Hope was about five, Julia had given her a gorgeous china tea set decorated with pink cabbage roses, complete with tiny plates and silverware, so she could join them from time to time. Or have tea parties with her stuffed animals, which she did quite often.

As she knocked on the door and heard Julia call out that she'd be right there, a little dagger of guilt jabbed at her. She'd been cool to Julia since she arrived. And she hadn't admitted to herself the real reason why. At first, it had been so difficult to see her mother's best friend beside her father. Without her mother there. And though her mom had asked Julia to keep an eye on her dad, there was obviously more to their relationship than that, she was quite sure of it. Or perhaps she was just reading more into it than was truly there. Julia had been a widow since Hope was in grade school and she overheard her tell her mom during one of those afternoon teas that she had no interest in anyone else. Her Patrick had been the love of her life.

Just then the door opened.

"Oh, Hope," Julia said, clearly surprised.

"Hi, Julia, I was wondering if you might have time for a cup of tea."

She broke into a smile, her brown eyes crinkling. "Of course. Come in."

She followed Julia into her kitchen, still all blue and white as Hope remembered. A picture window overlooked her yard and a small table and chairs sat in front of it. A white hutch was filled with her collection of Delft pottery. Hope sat as Julia filled a shiny copper teakettle.

"Is that the kettle my mom gave you?"

Julia turned and smiled. "Yes, it's seen better days, but I can't seem to part with it. When I retired, the other teachers gave me an electric kettle that heats water so much faster. But … sometimes we don't need fast."

"You two certainly enjoyed your tea and talks."

"We did."

Julia sat then. "But that's not what you came over to talk about. I can see you've got something on your mind."

"I know Zach has been coming over with his schoolwork, and I want to thank you again for helping him."

"It's truly my pleasure, Hope. He's a wonderful boy, and very bright."

"Thanks. I just wondered, though, Julia … we haven't seen you at my dad's house in a few days. Since he went to the ER."

Julia looked down at her hands, fiddling with a birthstone

ring. "Well, I know Red needs to take it easy now."

"Is that all? Really?"

Just then the kettle began to whistle. Julia got up and fetched cups, sugar and creamer, then sat and poured their tea. She took her time and Hope could see she was weighing her words carefully. After they finished fixing their cups, Julia finally looked up at her.

"Your father is upset with me."

"Because of what you told me?"

Julia nodded, then stirred her tea again.

"I tried to talk to him, but he refused," Hope said.

"That man! He can be so stubborn!"

"Oh, you don't have to tell me." Hope reached and took Julia's hand, squeezing. "I'm sorry. Truly."

Julia was shaking her head now, her emotions simmering. "He has let this fester for too long. Things don't go away just because you want them to! This ... thing between the two of you ... You deserve to know ... " She sighed, saying nothing more.

"Will you tell me, please? Obviously, you know. And I'm not sure I'll ever get him to open up to me."

Julia sighed, still shaking her head. "Oh, what the heck, he's already upset with me." She gazed out the window for a long moment, then turned to look straight at Hope. "I hear everyone in town is telling you stories about the star for your article. Well—"

"Wait," she interrupted. "I thought this was about my mom and dad."

"It is, Hope. I actually have a story about the star to tell you, though it's not really mine. It's your mom and dad's."

"Oh Julia, I'm sure I've heard it, then."

"Not this one, Hope."

Puzzled, she waited as Julia took a sip of tea.

"Your mom and dad were high school sweethearts."

"I know that," she said, anxious to get to whatever Julia was about to reveal.

"What you don't know is that when your mom went off to college, and your dad stayed here to take over the family hardware business, well, your mom met someone else."

Her mouth opened in shock.

"His name was Martin. I'll never forget him, he was so handsome, a sweet talker, had money, and traveled. He was like no one we'd met before, especially in a small town like this. And he was so smitten with your mom. He wanted to open up a whole new world for her. When he proposed, how could Alice say no?"

"What? Mom was engaged to someone else? How did I not know that?"

"Oh, Hope, I don't think she wanted you to."

"What happened then?"

"We were college roommates, remember? It was the end of our senior year and we were driving back to town one night in early May. Your Mom's car was all loaded up with our stuff. And, of course, with college over we were talking about our futures. What would come next for each of us. I'd already gotten a job lined up teaching here in town. She was talking about her wedding later that summer."

"Oh my ... she actually had the wedding all planned with

this guy?"

Julia nodded. "So, there we were, driving home. I just let her go on and on about the wedding details, the flowers, colors of bridesmaid dresses, her moving away ... and then as we were coming down the mountain into town, all of a sudden where the woods open up, your mom gasped. There was the Christmas Star on Buck Hill, shining across the valley."

"Wait ... but it was spring."

Julia nodded, smiling, and Hope could see she was back in that car, reliving that memory. "Yes, it was spring. First week of May to be exact. And your mom ... oh, Hope, she started to cry. She pulled the car over on the shoulder of the road and we sat there and she kept saying, 'But it's May, why is the star lit?'"

"And?"

"Oh, I knew Alice was confused, and having second thoughts though she never admitted as much. So ... without her knowing it, I helped your dad." She sat there with a sly smile on her face. "Your dad moved heaven and earth to get that star lit for her. You know your dad's never been much of a talker, or showy with things. Not like that Martin who'd swept her off her feet. But your dad convinced old Doc Stevens, who still lived up there at the time, to agree."

"I just can't believe this." She sat there, shaking her head, stunned. "Or that I never heard anything about it. So, what happened next?"

"As we sat there in the car, I handed your mom a note. It was from your dad. I'll never forget the look on her face as she opened it and read it aloud: *My love for you burns as bright as that star, Alice. It will never fade.*"

"Oh, Julia." Tears filled her eyes, imagining her parents in that moment. "That is the most beautiful story. And I can't believe my dad did all that."

"Your dad wanted her to see what she was really giving up. Not just him, but her friends and family. This town. He wanted her to see that *this* is where she belonged. This was home."

"*When you see the star, you'll know you're home.* I heard her say that my whole life." She paused and it was as if she could hear her mother's voice in Julia's kitchen. God, how she missed her.

As Julia got up and freshened their tea, giving her a moment, Hope sat there processing it all.

"I don't understand, though, what does this have to do with the rift between my dad and me?"

"Hope, you need to ask your father the rest. It's for him to tell you."

Julia got up as Hope sat there, staring out the picture window at the yard blanketed in snow. Her parents' history, which she thought she knew, was a completely different story from what she'd always believed. It was as romantic as a novel or a movie. She tried to imagine her father, who rarely showed emotion, putting all of his love into that heartfelt gesture. And in that incredible letter. *My love for you burns as bright as that star.* It was the stuff women dreamed of. He couldn't say the words, so he showed her his love in a different way. A way she couldn't miss.

She and Julia finished their tea and talked about Zach and how well he was doing with his lessons, despite missing school. When she left, she gave Julia a big hug, thanking her for everything. She was halfway back to her father's house when she stopped suddenly, as something began to come into focus. Something that might at least partially explain her father's behavior all those years ago.

CHAPTER 9

HOPE SPENT THE AFTERNOON UP in her old room, sitting on her twin bed with her computer on her lap, working on the star article. Occasionally she'd look out the window at Buck Hill, where the star was missing. After a while, she got up to stretch, then went and stood at the window, looking down at the garage where her dad, her son, and Ryan were still at it.

Just then she saw Ryan coming out the side door and going to his truck. He was limping a bit more, again. Yet he was still in there helping. He was so kind to Zach, and she could see he had great respect for her father. He was a good man. And he seemed to like her.

Or was he just being friendly because of her dad? She wondered what his relationship with Lauren really was. She seemed so possessive and it was clear she wanted him. Was it possible Phoebe was wrong and they were an item? Though he seemed a bit reticent with her. Although it just might be he was not comfortable with her making it so obvious in public.

Still, there were the moments he looked at her in a way

that was almost haunting. In the hospital, she thought he'd been about to kiss her. Or maybe she'd raised her mouth to his first, without realizing it? And now he asked her to the open mic tonight, and she was pretty sure his look wasn't just casual.

She shook her head to clear it. Why was she dwelling on any of this, anyway? None of it really mattered. She'd be gone soon. There was no point to starting anything here, even if there was actually something to start.

Without Julia coming by, Hope made sure to be downstairs to cook dinner. The guys, she knew, would be hungry after being out in the cold garage all afternoon. She kept it simple, tomato soup and grilled cheese sandwiches, her childhood favorite comfort food, and neither her dad nor Zach complained. Ryan had gone home, they explained.

"You guys don't mind if I go out for a little bit this evening, do you?" she asked as they were finishing up.

"Another Hometown Holiday meeting?" her dad asked.

"No, just, um, some of the gang are going to Mama's to hear some music, so I thought I might go."

"I think that's a wonderful idea, Honey. You've been doing nothing but working since you got here."

"You okay with that, Zach?"

He looked up from his soup, which he was clearly enjoying. "Sure, Mom. You should have some fun."

"And you two are done in the garage for the day, right?"

They looked at each other with a bit of a guilty look.

"I'm not going unless you promise."

"We promise," they said at the same time, then giggled.

"Okay, then."

She began cleaning up but her dad shooed her away.

"Go get ready," he said. "We've got this."

She went upstairs to change. She'd just go for an hour, she told herself, pushing aside a wave of guilt. She hadn't spent any real time with Zach since sledding a few days ago. Not that he seemed to mind. He was pretty busy himself between his schoolwork and the big project.

Maybe the break from everything would give her brain a chance to recharge. She remembered the old term from yoga, "monkey mind," and that's exactly how her head had been since she arrived. As though a dozen monkeys were constantly flitting from one thought, idea, or worry from moment to moment. She took a deep breath and let it out, hoping for a little while all the monkeys would vanish along with it.

Opening her old dresser drawer, she pulled out her red cashmere sweater, a holiday favorite. And then she stopped, holding it up. For the first time in years, she thought back to the moment she'd unwrapped this extravagant gift from Drew, one she'd never have bought for herself, the Christmas after they were married. She'd hugged and kissed him and even wore it that day when he took her to the best restaurant in town for their Christmas dinner. When they were on dessert, she'd slipped a little gift across the table to him.

"What's this? I thought we'd done the present thing this morning?" he asked, taken aback.

"Well ... " she'd begun, a bit nervous. "This is different. I didn't want it getting lost in the shuffle."

He began unwrapping the box with a little smile. When he lifted the top off, the smile disappeared. He held up the tiny yellow onesie. Her heart froze. Neither of them said a word for a long moment.

"I thought we agreed … "

"Yes, I know we said that we'd enjoy married life, travel more, before talking about babies again, but … it happened, Drew. It wasn't planned."

"I see."

"Wait … you believe me, don't you?"

He hesitated but then reached across the table for her hand and kissed it. "Of course, I believe you." In that moment of hesitation, though, she saw the doubt in his eyes. But she wasn't going to let anything dampen her joy. She was going to be a mother! Drew would come around.

She folded the red cashmere sweater, wondering why she'd held onto it for so long. Sure, it was beautiful. And she'd probably never be able to afford something like it again. But it was time to let it go.

Just then the college bells rang seven o'clock and she stopped her dawdling over the past and finished dressing, choosing jeans, a black turtleneck, rhinestone snowflake earrings she'd bought last Christmas, and her black suede boots. She went downstairs and put the red cashmere sweater into the box for donations. Hopefully, some lucky woman would get it for a song.

Then she went into the kitchen to get some decent snacks ready for the guys. When Hope walked into the family room five minutes later, her dad was beside Zach on the couch, a red plaid blanket on their laps, their feet up on the ottoman, ready to watch "Home Alone." Zach must have seen it a dozen times already, but still got a kick out of it.

She handed them the bowl. "Here's your popcorn, guys. Air-popped and heart healthy."

They both gave her a less than thrilled look.

"With a little butter and a smidge of salt, okay?"

They nodded in unison. She couldn't not smile. They were becoming quite the pair.

"Did you finish your article?" her dad asked.

"I'm getting there. I probably shouldn't even be going—"

"Go!" they shouted in unison.

"Okay! Nice to be wanted!" she laughed.

She pulled her coat on and as she walked out of the room, she turned to look at them on the couch, eating popcorn, watching the movie. Zach already whispering about his favorite part.

"Hey, you two, not too late, okay?"

"Ditto, Mom," Zach said, without looking away from the TV.

It was snowing so softly when she stepped outside that she decided to walk to Mama's. It was cold but there was no wind and it was so lovely to see all the houses in town lit up at night with their Christmas lights and snowmen and jolly Santas and reindeer. There was even Christmas music playing from some porches and she stopped for a moment to admire a blow-up snow globe with a carousel turning inside as it snowed all around it, and it reminded her of one she had as a kid.

When was the last time she'd done something like this? Go out on her own just to have fun?

Her life was so full of her work and her responsibilities with Zach and their home. And if she admitted it to herself, she could have taken more time for herself. But it always seemed unfair to Zach. Lily had tried to fix her up with how many guys, but she always said no. Her friends at work urged her to try online dating, but she refused. How could she do that to Zach? He was unhappy with his dad's revolving door of girlfriends. How could she take that chance herself? No, she'd resigned herself long ago that she wouldn't go there until he was much older. And she was fine with that, truly.

She could hear the music drifting from Mama's Café about half a block away. When she walked in, the place was crowded and festive, with Christmas lights strung throughout, tinsel garland draped around the doorways, and a gorgeous tree with miniature cooking utensils hung from the branches all lit up in the corner. A duo was singing on the small stage and she noticed a table in the corner where Phoebe was swaying to the music, wearing reindeer antlers. She also saw Jane in an ugly Christmas sweater, Norm in a Santa hat, and Lori in an elf costume, scattered between booths and mingling with others. As she headed toward them, her eyes scanned the room for Ryan.

"What a surprise!" Phoebe said, rushing toward her.

"Well, Ryan mentioned you guys would all be here."

Phoebe's eyebrows shot up and she flashed a smile.

"Stop!" Hope said. "He's a nice guy, yes, but ... I live hundreds of miles away."

"I wish you didn't. It's been like old times with you here."
Phoebe put an arm around her and put her head on her shoulder.
"Hey, this is perfect! Let's do 'Santa Baby' just like the old times!"

"Oh, no! I haven't sung in—"

But Phoebe was already dragging her to the stage. She
began giggling with embarrassment, her nerves kicking into
high gear. Before she knew it, they were on the stage, and she
looked out to see Ryan walking in. The music started and they
began singing, a bit hesitant at first, until Phoebe began belt-
ing it out and Hope winced, hearing herself off-key. Phoebe
pantomimed some of the verses as they sang, and Hope played
along, laughing now more than she was singing. A few times
she glanced at Ryan, who was smiling broadly, clearly enjoying
the show. When the song ended, the place erupted in cheers.
They took a little bow and left the stage in giggles.

"That was great!" Phoebe said, turning to her as they hit
the floor.

"Seriously? That was mortifying! I can't believe you talked
me into it. Actually, more like dragged me into it." But she was
still laughing. And she had to admit to herself, it was fun.

As they headed toward Phoebe's booth, Ryan came
toward her.

"I hope you didn't listen too closely to that."

"Actually, I'm impressed. You're a good writer *and* a pretty
decent singer."

"Well, I'm not sure decent would be accurate for my singing. But how would you know I'm a good writer?"

"I googled you and I read some of your features in
the *Tribune.*"

134

"Oh?" She was quite surprised.

"You're really talented. I particularly liked the piece you wrote about the endangered loggerhead turtles. I learned a lot from it, but it wasn't preachy."

"Thank you. We don't live far from the beach and the loggerheads nest every summer there and have become more and more at risk with development."

"I found it really moving that the mother loggerhead comes all the way back to the beach where she was born, sometimes thousands of miles away, to hatch her own young."

"Wow, you really read closely."

He gave her a long look and she felt her face begin to grow warm. "I did."

Just then Norm came over to them and tapped Ryan on the shoulder. "Hey, buddy, want to back me on 'Jingle Bell Rock?'"

"Sure thing. I'll be right there."

"Wait, you're a musician?"

Ryan shrugged. "I just play a little harmonica, nothing big. Will you excuse me for a bit?"

"Of course."

She watched him as he went over to a table and opened a case, then walked onto the stage with Norm, who was carrying a guitar. They warmed up for a few minutes and then Norm began to strum and sing, with Ryan playing a killer harmonica. Everyone began to dance, including Phoebe and the gang, who kept waving for her to join them. But Hope stood there watching Ryan, his eyes closed, his lips sliding back and forth on the harmonica. The man was certainly full of surprises.

The song ended and Ryan left the stage as Norm began

a slow and bluesy "Blue Christmas." Couples broke out onto the dance floor now, including Phoebe and her husband, Jim, who'd just arrived. Ryan was putting his harmonica away when Phoebe called out, "Hey you two, get out here! It's Christmas!"

Ryan looked at her and their eyes locked. He held out his hand. "Shall we do this?"

"I'd like that."

He put an arm around her waist, drawing her close, as his other hand took hers and they began moving slowly to the music. He was looking down at her, his eyes searching, and she couldn't seem to look away as much as she tried. His arm tightened, pulling her closer, her mouth now just inches from his. She felt her lips moving toward his and she couldn't stop herself. It was okay, her mind was telling her. It's the holidays, it's just a fun interlude. As his lips nearly brushed hers the song ended and a rousing applause jolted them from the moment. She stepped away from him quickly.

"How about a drink?" Ryan asked, his voice husky.

"That ... that would be great." She walked over to his booth and sat down across from him. A waitress came over and took their order. She was having a hard time pulling herself away from the moment they shared.

"I ... I want to thank you again for everything you've done with Zach. Sleigh riding and ... the garage project." She wouldn't let it slip she knew it was a float. After first telling her, Zach seemed to have forgotten and kept mysteriously calling it his 'project.' "I haven't seen him this excited in a long time."

"Well, the project was actually Zach's idea. He's pretty excited about it."

"Any hints?"

"Just that you're going to be quite surprised. And impressed. I'm happy to help."

The waitress set down his beer and her wine and they raised and touched glasses.

"Did you get things straightened out with Zach's dad for the holidays?"

"I think so. He's agreed now to come to South Carolina and get Zach and fly with him back to California to meet up with his girlfriend and all fly together to Hawaii."

"Good. I'm glad."

"I just hope he sticks to it. Drew has a way of … oh shall we say springing last-minute surprises that suit no one but him."

Ryan shook his head. "Zach deserves better."

"I know."

"And how about you and your dad?"

"I'm glad you asked. Remember that night in the hospital when I said that I needed to talk to my dad—"

"You don't need to go into that, Hope."

"No, it's okay. Believe it or not, my rift with my dad began years ago. After my mom passed, when I told him I was going to marry Drew, he was completely against it. My dad thought he was wrong for me and, well, Drew and I eventually eloped. I couldn't understand why he acted the way he did, because my mother would have been supportive. I know she wanted to see me settled in life and that would've brought her comfort."

"I'm sorry, that must have been rough."

"It was. But time went by quickly after we married and moved away and the distance between us just grew. I shouldn't have let that happen. I was an idiot. And dad, well he kind of held a grudge for way too long and ... it's complicated but I feel awful about it now. And there's more, apparently, on his side, according to Julia, but he's been avoiding talking."

"I think you're probably doing a good job making up for it now. As I said, your dad seems like a different guy from when I first met him."

"I'm glad to hear that. I have a lot to make up for. He was right, really. If I'd given it more time, I probably would have seen Drew's true colors."

"You can't blame yourself for trying to see the best in someone. I think that's just who you are, Hope."

She smiled. "Thank you, that's kind of you to say. So, what about you? Have you ever been married, or ... "

"I was engaged once."

"Oh?"

Ryan hesitated.

"I'm sorry, I shouldn't—"

But he put a hand up. "It's okay, it was a while ago. We met a year into my last tour and we were supposed to get married when that tour was over and I returned back to the States, but ... well, I got hurt then and ... " he shrugged. "Turns out it was more than she wanted to deal with."

"Oh, Ryan, how awful. I'm so sorry."

"Don't be. She wasn't really who I thought she was, obviously. You're certainly not alone in that mistake. I wanted a simple life, you know? A house, kids, a dog ... well, I did get the dog." He gave a little laugh but it held no humor."

"And that's why you bought the house on Buck Hill?"

"I looked for a few years. When I found it, I liked the privacy, the woods, the view of the town below. And the people seemed friendly. It just seemed like a good place to figure out the next part of my life. I'd been in the Marines for so long, the real world seemed a bit ... I don't know, I guess unreal, if that makes sense."

"It does, yes. And I think you've done a great job here. You're part of this town now. I think you're even starting to like Christmas a little bit," she said, the last part in a teasing tone.

He laughed, shaking his head, not disagreeing. Just then the music stopped and Norm was back on the mic. "We have a request for 'Silent Night' by Mr. Ryan Miller on the harmonica. Ryan, you still here?"

Ryan looked at her, then stood up, unzipping his harmonica case. "Excuse me again."

"Of course," she said, watching him once again walk to the stage, sit on a stool, then pull his harmonica to his lips.

He closed his eyes again and began a slow and haunting rendition of the hymn that brought the room to stillness. Tears filled her eyes, imagining him as a little boy in foster care, bounced from home to home, never having a real Christmas. And now the man, wounded not just in war, but in love. He was a good man. She had no doubt of that. And if only the timing and the distance were different it would be easy to fall for him. He was unlike any man she'd known. But her focus had to be Zach, and her job and a new home that would make this next move as easy as possible on her son. Because at the end of the day, no matter how she felt about a man, Zach would always come first.

Ryan offered to walk her back to her dad's house, which she refused, thinking of his leg. But he kept insisting. Truthfully, she hadn't really wanted the night to end. For a little while, she'd forgotten about all of her cares. She'd laughed harder than she had in years. And it was nice to be looked at like a woman again.

Their conversation was light during the walk and they began rating the decorations as if it were an Olympic sport, giving the classic houses high marks and laughing at an over-decorated house that looked like Clark Griswold's. They even passed a house with a Star Wars Christmas theme that had them howling. And another where the lights on the house blinked in time to music playing from speakers on the lawn.

Soon they were in front of her father's house, with its white snowflake lights hanging from the eaves, a colorful wreath on the front door, and a beautiful nativity scene in front of the dogwood. She paused a moment, as did he, admiring its simple beauty.

"Thanks for walking me back, especially since you now have to walk all the way back to Mama's to get your truck. Or I could give you a lift?"

"No, that's not necessary. The places I've lived you never let a lady walk alone in the dark. Not that Hackettstown is like that. But I actually like walking in the snow after all those years spent in the desert."

"I just feel bad ... " she said, nodding toward his leg.

"Listen, my leg works pretty good. Does everything I need

it to do. And … they weren't even sure I was going to keep it, so I kind of like this leg, as imperfect as it is. I can handle a little limp and some aches from time to time."

"Oh, Ryan."

He suddenly seemed uncomfortable, as if he'd said too much. "Well, I better get going. We have a long day tomorrow in the garage finishing up."

"Thanks again for inviting me. It was really fun."

He didn't move. Suddenly he reached over and brushed snow from her hair, staring at her. Her heart went still, waiting. Then he backed away and nodded.

"I guess I'll see you tomorrow then."

She nodded. "Good night, Ryan."

"Good night, Hope."

She stood there watching until he disappeared down the street.

It was late that night and Hope was sitting on the attic floor, surrounded by boxes again and looking out the tiny attic window, thinking. Zach and her dad were asleep when she'd gotten back from Mama's so she figured she'd get something accomplished, as she wasn't sleepy at all. She'd barely gotten started when she heard footsteps and soon saw her father's head coming up the attic stairs. He was wearing his old green flannel robe. She thought to herself once again how much frailer he was beginning to look. Or maybe he was just tired.

"There you are," he said, coming over to where she sat on the floor. "I didn't hear you come in."

"I thought you were both asleep so I tried to be quiet."

"I couldn't sleep." He sat on a trunk. "You're up really late. Is everything okay?"

"Oh, I've been trying to finish my articles but my mind's been elsewhere. I was actually sitting here thinking about Mom."

He smiled, shaking his head. "She'd have loved Zach, Honey. I wish she'd gotten to … " He stopped, the catch in his voice obvious. Hope's own eyes filled and neither of them spoke again for a long moment.

"Dad, Julia told me a story today. How you got the star lit for mom when she came home from college and … and was about to marry someone else."

Her father looked up at the ceiling, rolling his eyes, clearly upset.

"Dad, please, I deserve to know the truth. Don't you think enough time has gone by?"

He got up, walked across the room, and she thought he was leaving. Then he turned back to her and sighed. "Oh, Hope, your mom loved you so much. She only wanted the best for you. Her little girl."

"I know, Dad."

"When you brought Drew home, she was so afraid you were about to make the same mistake she almost did. Drew reminded her of … that other guy." He came over and sat on the trunk again. He seemed overcome with emotion. "Honey, your mom thought Drew was self-centered and that he'd never put you first. He didn't even seem to want kids. And your dream of writing? That seemed like a lark to him, implying there wouldn't be much money in it. As if that should discount your talent."

"I didn't know she felt that way. I thought she actually liked him."

"Honey, he just didn't see you the way we did. Especially your mom. She was so proud of your writing. Why, do you remember the article you wrote in 4th grade about the star?"

"I do, Dad. I actually found it up here last week. It's kind of been inspiring me."

"Do you know what she said back then when you read it to us out loud? She told me that she truly believed you had a real gift. And then when she thought you might stop writing … because of him, or not even have children … it seemed you'd be giving up so much of yourself. She was so afraid of that happening."

"So then after she died, when I told you I wanted to marry Drew and you put your foot down and forbade me … it was really her?"

He nodded. "Honey, you have to understand. Your mom knew she wasn't going to be here for you, to talk to you, to help you see he might be exciting and offer lots of things, but in the end, he wasn't right for you. She made me promise I would do everything I could to prevent it. Hope, I knew you'd be upset and angry."

He was right. She'd been furious with him, taking away the little happiness she'd found after the heartache of losing her mother. "But why didn't you just tell me the truth?"

"You were grieving over your mom and then he had you blinded with excitement and travel, and I just … I couldn't bear to have you upset at her. She wasn't even here to explain it to you."

"So you took the fallout. Oh, Dad."

She got up from the floor and walked over to the window, her mind reeling. Remembering how much her heart hurt. How it seemed as though the earth should have stopped spinning, because how could it go on without her mother? And then Drew began talking about marriage and it was something to hang onto, pulling her toward a new future, one away from the pain of her loss. An exciting life of travel and living in New York City where he worked. A life that seemed, at the time, like a fairy tale. And then her father had pulled the rug out from under it all, and the big wedding turned into an elopement. But now ... now she knew it wasn't really him. It was her mother who saw the mistake she might make, like the one she almost did, but wouldn't be here to stop it.

"Oh, Dad. All this time I've been upset thinking I've disappointed you and ... you were just following her wishes. You were protecting mom. And she was right!"

He nodded and Hope put her head in her hands. "I've been such an idiot. I'm so sorry, Dad."

"Honey," her dad said softly, "it doesn't matter anymore. What matters is you're here and I've got this amazing grandson. That's the good that came out of it. And you're still writing."

She walked over then, knelt on the floor and hugged her father. "I'm so sorry, Dad," she whispered. He held her a long time until she sat back on her heels, her eyes filled with tears again. "Dad, I was so ashamed, and honestly, I was more mad at myself because you were right. Drew didn't want kids, but then Zach came along and I thought it would change things, but he was still so selfish. And when he saw my checks for writing, he'd actually laugh. I felt like such a failure."

"You are no failure!"

"I think part of me staying away was also that I just couldn't bear coming back with Mom not here. That was selfish of me. And then that led to guilt and after a while, it just got too hard."

"Listen, Honey, if I've learned anything since your mom left us it's that grief is a process and you can't force it away. I should have reached out and tried more after you eloped. But I think I was just so lost in my own grief. Do you know I was mad at your mom for a long time for leaving us?"

"Oh, Dad."

"How crazy is that? As if she'd ever willingly leave us. But one day you begin to wake up from the grieving and ... suddenly years have gone by. I think maybe that's what happened with you and me, in our own ways."

"I promise you this, Dad. Even after Zach and I go back to South Carolina, we will visit often."

Her father nodded, but he didn't look happy.

"And you'll be in Florida soon, so you'll be even closer to us and we'll come see you there."

Now he gave a little smile.

"But please, don't be mad at Julia. You and I are so stubborn we may never have gotten here without her push. Right?"

"She meant well. I know that."

"Good. I think she's hurting right now. You two have obviously become such good friends."

"We have, yes."

"And Dad, that story about you and Mom and the star …
it's just incredible. Now I understand why she always said it:
When you see the star, you'll know you're home."

CHAPTER 10

THE FOLLOWING MORNING, HOPE DROVE Zach up to Ryan's workshop. Before the car even stopped, Ryan came outside with Kodi at his heels wagging his tail at the sight of Zach.

"Good morning," he called out.

"Good morning," she said, blushing a bit as she remembered last night and how close they'd come to kissing. "My dad got called to the store and asked me to bring Zach up to work on something with you."

Ryan seemed all business now as they followed him into the workshop. The woodstove was heating up the space nicely and the place smelled of freshly brewed coffee. Zach took his coat off. Now Kodi was at his side, following his every step.

"Would you like a cup of coffee," Ryan asked, picking up the pot that was on top of the woodstove. "I just made it."

"Oh, I can't stay, I've got too much writing to finish."

"Say no more." he said, with a half-smile.

Of course, he didn't ask anything further. He knew what she was writing. And she knew he preferred not to talk about it. She turned to her son. "Zach, did you remember something you have in your pocket?"

"Oh, right, Mom."

Zach turned to Kodi who began to whine with excitement as he pulled a treat from his pocket. "Kodi, sit," Zach commanded, his palm up, just as she'd seen Ryan do.

The dog sat obediently and Zach held out the biscuit. She was surprised at how delicately Kodi took the biscuit into his mouth. He was a big dog and she'd worried Zach's fingers might get nibbled.

"Good boy, Kodi," Ryan said.

"So, what is it you guys are up to this morning," she asked.

"Mom, stop! It's a surprise, part of our project."

She looked over at Ryan, who smiled for real now, then shrugged as if to say *Don't look at me.*

"Okay, then, I'll leave you guys to it. Just let me know when to pick him up, okay?"

"I'll just bring him back down to your dad's when we're finished," Ryan said. "I've got more work in the attic to do later on."

"Ditto that," she said.

Driving back down Buck Hill, she found her thoughts drifting again and again to Ryan, as they'd been since the night before. Was he just being nice to her and Zach because of her dad? Or was he really interested in her? Her opinion jumped back and forth. There was no denying they'd come close to kissing several times. But maybe it was just being lost in the moment, the magic and romance of the holidays. She'd been out of the dating game for so long, she had no clue anymore.

So maybe it was okay to just flirt a bit and enjoy this interlude. If she was being honest with herself, she was enjoying it. It really was nice to feel like a woman again. Besides, she'd be back to home and reality soon enough. And the thought of that sent a little wave of dread through her.

As she pulled into the driveway and glanced at the dashboard clock, she realized she was down to just hours to finish both articles. She'd be moving in six or seven weeks, but to where? And what if she couldn't find another rental in Zach's school district? He loved his teachers, and all his friends were there. Worse yet, what if she didn't keep her job? Her savings would only carry them for perhaps six months. And she'd never, ever turn to Drew. He made it no secret that he thought her salary working for a newspaper was a joke. There wasn't a lot of money in writing, that was true, but it was what she was born to do, she knew that now. And there was more to life than just money. Somehow she always found a way to manage.

But right now, she had to focus. It was crunch time and she needed to start writing. Hopefully, Phoebe's prediction would hold true. That the pressure of these last hours would somehow force her best work out of her once again.

The house was too quiet, so Hope put some soothing spa music on her phone and sat with a cup of jasmine tea at the kitchen island, where she had a lovely view of the yard, all snow-covered with the big old blue spruce lit with colored lights reflecting on its snowy branches. She opened her laptop and began to type. Two articles due in a matter of hours. One would hopefully bring back the star. And one would hopefully clinch keeping her job. But the one that seemed to come to life as she sat there was her star article. So she continued working on that one, hoping that by the time she finished with it, the other article, which seemed to be the polar opposite, would somehow begin to take root.

By lunchtime she was still in the kitchen, figuring Zach would be back anytime and they could eat together. But he wasn't back yet. As she was warming up some leftover beef barley soup, her father walked in.

"I thought I'd come home for lunch today if you don't mind. But I don't want to interrupt your writing. I know you're down to the wire now."

"No, it's fine, I was just taking a break for lunch. Let me heat some up for you, as well."

She heated him a bowl of beef barley and got out the saltines and butter, which she knew he loved with his soup. "Dad, have you talked to Julia yet?"

He shook his head sheepishly.

"This isn't going to go away, Dad. I think you need to just bite the bullet and go over and talk to her."

He sighed. "I acted like a jerk."

With her back to him, she allowed herself a little smile. "We all do at times. But your intentions weren't malicious, Dad, right? That's the important thing. You two have shared a lot and obviously become good friends." And now she turned to face him. "Or is it more than that?"

Her father actually blushed. "Don't be silly. Julia was your mom's best friend."

"So what? She's a wonderful woman and you've been alone for so long now. I think—"

"Stop! I'm fine. I don't mind being alone."

"Okay, okay."

She put his bowl on the table and sat and they ate in silence for a while.

"Dad, how long have you known Ryan?"

"Oh, I guess a few years. He came into the store shortly after moving here for lots of things to fix up the workshop. Why?"

"I was just wondering."

Her dad gave her a long look. "He's a good man, Hope. And I see the way he looks at you."

"Now you stop," she said with a little laugh. "I have no time for that. I'm leaving soon and my focus is on Zach."

"You deserve a life, too, Honey."

She shook her head. "Not now. Zach is too young."

She put her bowl in the dishwasher then picked up her laptop and notes. "I need a change of scenery. I think I'll go upstairs and sit on my bed to work for a bit."

"And look up at the star? I mean where it should be?"

She nodded. She was at the point where she needed inspiration. And looking out that window ... it never failed to move her.

Ten minutes later as she sat on her bed, her computer on her lap and pages spread all around her, she was doing just that, gazing out the window. Willing that empty space on top of Buck Hill to speak to her. But then her eye caught a figure moving below, across the yard. She got up and looked down to see her father walking through the side yard to Julia's back door. She smiled, then turned and got back on the bed and pulled her laptop on top of the blanket.

Red saw Julia through her kitchen window as he went to her back door. He stopped a moment, just watching her. There was something so lovely about her at her stove, stirring a pot, her cheeks flushed from the steam, her silver hair tied back in a little bun, completely unaware of being seen.

Julia was as different from Alice as night and day. Where Julia was comfortable just going with the flow, a bit of a free spirit, Alice was always in control of everything, with lists in her purse and sticky notes on the fridge. And she had to be, always taking on more than she could handle. The Hometown Holiday became the Spring Festival a few months later, and then the town's Oktoberfest in the Fall, which she didn't run, but did more than her fair share for. She volunteered for everything when Hope was in school, from room mother to chaperone on class trips, to bake sales and tricky trays. In addition to coaching Hope in middle school basketball, she taught Sunday School and cooked for the priests. And she'd been his designer and creator for his annual Christmas wreaths that sold like hotcakes, starting them at the kitchen table before Thanksgiving. Her beautiful spring and summer baskets of flowers began in March with Easter bulbs and always sold out a week before the holiday. How many times had he asked her to slow down, that she was taking on too much. But it was her joy, and he couldn't stop her. And like a bright light, she began to dim until it was too late.

After decades of teaching boisterous second graders, Julia

loved her quiet time. "I earned this," she'd say about her long afternoons reading on the porch, or savoring a sunset as she sat with a glass of wine in the yard. Once, when someone asked what her favorite thing to do was, she'd said "Nothing. I love retirement." She was the only one who could slow Alice down. Their girl time was something special.

Since Hope came, Julia had been busier than usual, but she seemed happy to do it. Helping Zach with his schoolwork. Cooking meals for all of them and baking Christmas cookies. He wondered what she was making now. She had her reading glasses perched halfway down her nose, so she could see what she was cooking. On top of her head sat her prescription glasses, for distance. She couldn't seem to get the hang of progressives, so one pair could suit all her needs. They often laughed about her lost pairs of glasses, especially when she'd be looking for the pair that sat right on top of her head.

Oh, he could relate to that. And that was the thing. The bond, really. They had so much in common. Lost spouses, though her Patrick had been gone for decades now. The little trials of aging that they could laugh about, and could have easily gone the other way. At first, a few years ago, when he began to realize his feelings of friendship were shifting to something more serious, he'd held himself back. It had felt, at the time, like a betrayal of Alice.

But they both loved Alice. And she was often in their conversations, their joint memories. And once he made peace with that, he began to allow himself to feel something more. He knew, though, that Julia had never gotten over Pat's death. He'd been so young and she could have easily married again, but she never did.

Now, though, the only thing he knew with certainty was that he had to make things right with Julia. She was a good woman. She had stood by his side after Alice's death. After Hope left. Somehow, she'd nudged him back to the real world. And she'd asked so little in return.

It was almost harder to think of leaving her behind than it was to leave Hackettstown. But last year, with his daughter and grandson so far away, the long, bitter winters causing his bones to ache, and knowing he'd have a reduced income when he'd finally retire, moving south had seemed like the right decision. He had made a plan then and he'd put it in place. And now the time was almost here. Ryan would be finished with his repairs in January and then he planned to put his house on the market for spring. It was all falling into place.

Except now things were different, in so many ways. And if he was honest with himself, he needed to not just apologize to Julia. He needed to finally tell her how he really felt about her.

Hope woke to the sound of a buzz saw, no doubt coming from the garage. Opening her eyes, she saw the room was nearly dark. Outside, dusk was falling quickly. Oh no, she'd been sleeping for several hours. This was not good, not with her deadlines. She took her computer and gathered up her pages and went downstairs to start a pot of coffee, still groggy. While waiting, she sat at the counter and opened her laptop to where she'd left off. By the time the coffee was ready, she was starting to get back into the groove. Before she knew it, the back door opened and in walked Zach, followed by her dad and Ryan. They were high-fiving and laughing until they saw her and suddenly got quiet, giving each other warning looks.

"Okay, what are you three up to?" she teased.

"Mom, I told you, it's a surprise!" Zach said.

"You'll find out soon enough, Hope," her father chastised.

"I'm starving," Zach announced, taking off his coat.

"Oh … " she'd forgotten all about supper. She jumped up. "Let me see what I can whip up quickly."

"No worries," her dad said. "Julia's coming over at six-thirty with a casserole. She wants you to have plenty of time to keep working on your article."

"Oh! Okay," she said, smiling. Obviously, they'd made peace.

"I'll just grab my tools in the attic and head out then," Ryan said, walking across the kitchen to the foyer to go up to the attic.

"Nonsense, Julia made plenty and specifically said to ask you. Do you like Shepherd's Pie?"

"Mmm, that's hard to say no to."

"It's settled then," her dad said, with a satisfied smile. He seemed more relaxed than she'd seen him since she arrived.

"All right," Ryan said. "I'll just get started on that final section of the attic then until dinner."

"If you're not worn out, sure," her dad said with a little laugh.

"No worries, it's just a lot of measuring for now."

"Okay, Ryan. Now Zach and I have a puzzle to finish in the family room."

155

Her dad left with her son, conveniently leaving her alone with Ryan.

"How's it going with your writing?"

She was surprised he asked. "Kind of like one step forward, two steps back. I was going to go upstairs and work some more, but I think I'm ready for a break. Would you like a beer, or a glass of wine?"

"A beer sounds good," he said, sitting at the island.

She poured herself a glass of red wine and him a beer. "I'm feeling guilty that Zach is spending so much time with you guys while I'm buried in ... everything," she laughed.

"He's enjoying himself, don't worry."

"Hey," she said suddenly, "have you ever made Christmas cookies? You know the kind you ice and decorate that look like little works of art and you hate to eat them?"

"Can't say that I have. I think just the simple kind, like chocolate chips."

"Well, that's what I'm planning to do with Zach tomorrow after my deadlines to keep from stressing out after sending in my articles. My mother always said there's no problem in the world that won't feel a little bit easier after a good cookie."

"Your mother was a wise woman."

"That she was." She got up and began rooting through the cupboards to make sure she had all the ingredients she'd need. Then she opened the pantry, and there were her mother's cookbooks, still lined up. She pulled one out.

"So, if they look like works of art, do you get to eat them?"

"Of course. And they taste like heaven. Best of all, it's so much fun for kids. And grownups, believe it or not. You can get very creative." She opened the cookbook to pages of colorful and intricate cookies. "These are all Christmas cookies. The ones with the messiest pages are my favorites. I love those little blotches of flour or greasy fingerprints you know were from mixing dough with your hands. It's like little artifacts of those moments I spent baking with my mother." She closed her eyes for a moment, as a wave of emotion hit her.

"You okay?"

She nodded. "I would give anything to have one more day with her. Even one more minute."

"I can imagine."

She looked up, realizing how thoughtless her words were. "I'm sorry, I know you didn't—"

But he quickly put a hand up. "It's okay. We did bake cookies at the base when we had downtime. Nothing as elaborate as what you made, but ... they were pretty tasty."

"I didn't really mean the cookies, Ryan. I got to have my mother for almost two decades. You didn't even—"

"I know, Hope," he said, stopping her. "Really, it's okay. You have a good heart. I know you'd never do anything intentionally to hurt anyone."

"Thank you. I feel the same way about you."

He smiled.

Maybe it was a good time to take a gamble, while he was being so open, and considerate.

"Ryan, can I show you something?"

"Your favorite cookies of all?" he asked, smiling.

"No, something different. Something that might help you understand about ... what I'm writing."

His smile faded. "Sure."

"Come upstairs with me for a minute."

She gathered her laptop and pages and went upstairs as Ryan followed. She set her things on her bed and walked to the window. "Here," she nodded to him.

He came and stood beside her.

"There," she said, pointing up to the top of Buck Hill.

His gaze followed hers. Neither of them spoke for a long minute.

"All my life when I lived here, that's what I saw from this window, just darkness. But in December, which I waited for all year long, the star would be lit, glowing in the night like it was hanging up in the sky. It was magical. And every night I'd lay in my bed over there and stare up at it, sometimes for hours. And I'd make wishes."

He closed his eyes, sighing.

"It's not just me, Ryan. Everyone in town looks to that star as ... oh, a symbol that there's always hope, no matter the situation. It just brings comfort. And maybe a little bit of a feeling that anything is possible. But to have that place dark now ... it's really sad."

He turned to her then. "Hope, I don't want to disappoint you, but it's not possible. I didn't intend to take this on when I moved into that house. I was just looking for ... as I said, a place to start over. Sometimes things change, and we have to adapt. So maybe down the road something else will fill that void."

"I understand about things changing and adapting, trust me." She knew what he was talking about, of course, his injury. "But sometimes there's a chance you have to take to get what you really want."

"I thought you'd given up on this. That you were working on a different article."

"No," she said, surprised. "Well, I should be, yes, for the *Tribune* back home, but … this is the one I feel inside. And now, it feels like it's writing itself. The words are coming from this part of me I've kind of forgotten. Until I came back. That's what the star does."

"I can't fix it."

"But I'm trying to tell you, it's not yours to take on. If we can raise the money and hire the people … "

But he was already turning away.

She stood there at the window as he walked out the door.

It was late when Ryan opened his workshop door with Kodi at his heels. He began walking to his house. It was a frigid, clear night and he paused, glancing up to a black velvet sky studded with thousands of stars. Some people hated the cold or simply tolerated winter. But for him, there was stark beauty in all of it. The sky was never this vivid, even in the summer. And the bare trees standing like sentinels at attention in the woods surrounding him were draped in snow now like works of art, especially now at night when they took on an otherworldly beauty. He turned and through the woods, he could see the lights of the town below him. For a moment he tried to imagine all of those people looking up here in anticipation. Waiting for their beloved star to be lit.

He hadn't stayed for dinner after all with Hope and her

family. How could he? When he left her bedroom to go upstairs and get the rest of his tools, he thought he still might stay. But when he came back down from the attic, he'd opened the door to the upstairs hall and froze. Right across the hall, Hope's bedroom door was also open. She was sitting on her bed surrounded by papers, her computer in front of her. She looked up at him, her face lit by the screen of her laptop and a small lamp on the wall behind her. There was something almost intimate in the moment, and even before, when he'd stood there with her in her old bedroom, pleading with him to bring back the star. But he saw the disappointment on her face then and realized he couldn't stay. The last thing he ever wanted to do was hurt her.

He turned now in the bitter cold to look up at the sad remains of the star that still stood. He tried to imagine it fixed again, shining as it once did over the town. There must've been hundreds of lights at one time, maybe even several thousand. He tried to picture it repaired and ready to be lit. What would that moment be like, when it was suddenly illuminated? As he stared for a long time, his eyes began to blur, then hurt. He closed them, squeezing them shut, then opening them. Suddenly it was as if it were really happening, the star bursting into bright light and instantly blinding him as bulbs exploded, searing his eyes as he sank to his knees, the roar of blasts whirling all around him. Panic squeezed at his lungs until he couldn't draw breath. He began to gasp, he couldn't see. He began to scream, covering his head with his hands to drown out the screams all around him.

Then something was pushing him. Kodi. The dog began

to whine and lick his hands. He began the slow breathing he'd learned long ago, forcefully counting in and out, keeping to the rhythm, his heart gradually easing.

"It's okay, boy. I'm okay," he managed minutes later.

He was cold suddenly, as the sweat of fear began to dry on him. Kodi nudged him again, his snout trying to work his hands free from his face. He reached over to his dog, stroking him, his hand shaking violently. Kodi began licking his face.

"Come on, boy," he said, getting up finally. "Let's go home."

CHAPTER 11

HOPE HEARD A NOISE AND opened her eyes. Her father was standing above her with a blanket.

"I was just about to cover you. I'm sorry I woke you."

"Oh, no it's okay," she said, stretching.

"Were you up all night?"

She looked over at the family room window to see it was getting light outside.

"Well, I guess I fell asleep at some point." Suddenly a jolt of excitement hit her, then suddenly fizzled. "Dad, I finished my star article. I sent it in late last night. I've got the stories, the memories, the history, and I think I've captured what the star means to this town."

He sat on the coffee table and took her hand, squeezing. "That's wonderful, Honey. But … why don't you sound more excited?"

"I've been trying to write my other article for the *Tribune*. It's due this morning. I stayed awake for hours trying to finish it after I finished the star piece, but … I've got nothing. Nothing good enough anyway."

"I'm sure you're just being too hard on yourself."

"No, Dad. It's like my heart isn't really in it."

"Maybe you're just exhausted. You've been burning the candle at both ends and then some."

"It's not that." She shook her head and sighed. "Maybe it's the pressure. It's going to mean keeping my job. Or losing it. And every time I get started, I feel like I choke."

"Hope, you know what your mom would tell you, don't you?"

She looked at her dad and smiled. "I know. Don't lose hope. Things always work out for a reason."

"Somehow they always seemed to."

"Yes, they did."

"Do you remember when you were working on that speech you gave for high school graduation?"

"Yes, and the night before I was still working on it at midnight and I was just choking then, too."

"And?"

"She told me to write from my heart. And that it would all work out."

Her dad nodded.

"I wish she was here."

"Me, too, Honey."

She got up and gathered her things. "I'm going to shower and try to wake up. Do you think you can keep an eye on Zach?"

"Of course. Julia was planning to come over and finish up some of his schoolwork so take your time."

"Thanks, Dad."

The sky was heavy and dark gray clouds raced above the valley, obscuring the ring of mountains surrounding Hackettstown, when Hope got into her car. She backed out of the driveway and then drove toward Buck Hill, turning onto the private lane a few minutes later. Fog rose up from the snow-covered ground and the trees were shrouded in mist. She drove slowly up the curved, steep road and every once in a while, caught a deer standing frozen in the woods, watching her.

She pulled into Ryan's driveway, got out of the car and walked toward his workshop. She paused at a large stack of lumber that wasn't there the last time she'd been here. Then she heard the whine of a saw and looked in the window. She could see Ryan at his workbench, slipping a piece of curved wood from under the saw, then stroking it, as though it were something precious. It looked like an angel's wing. He picked it up then and took it to another table and lay it beside the metal angel ornament that had just one wing. His limp was barely noticeable and she imagined it was because it was early in the day and his leg wasn't tired yet.

Gently he held the wing so that the angel now had two. Her heart softened, watching him piece it together so reverently. A moment later, he walked back to his workbench and she knocked on the door before walking inside. Ryan looked up in surprise.

"I hope I'm not interrupting," she said.

"Not at all. I was just putting the final touches on the angel. The last of the ornaments to be repaired. She will go on the corner of Main and Moore," and now he looked at her with raised eyebrows, "*exactly* where you showed me."

"Okay, thank you for paying attention. Just trying to keep the tradition alive." She came closer to the ornament. "What happened to her wings?"

Ryan came closer and pointed to the metal she was made of. "If you look carefully, you'll see how fragile the metal is. Those wings wouldn't have lasted in any wind, so I made new ones."

"You're putting wood on metal?"

He shrugged. "It's not what one would normally do, but it's a quick fix. The Hometown Holiday starts tonight and I've got too much else to do to take time for welding. It'll do for now."

"It's perfect," she said.

"Oh, it's far from perfect, but ... there's really nothing perfect in this world."

She nodded. Of course, there wasn't. "Well, it's certainly clever."

"Sometimes you just have to make do with what you have."

He gave her a long look and now she wasn't sure if he was talking about his leg, or if he was again talking like last night about the star.

She decided to change the subject. "So, what's with all the lumber outside?"

"I'm expanding the workshop. Business is growing."

"Well good for you. My father seems to think you're the best carpenter he's ever met. And he doesn't throw compliments around."

"Are you trying to butter me up, Hope," he said then with

165

a teasing smile.

But suddenly she couldn't make light of any of this anymore. She unzipped her bag and took out several sheets of paper that were clipped together and handed them to him.

"I wanted to give you my article about the star. It went live online last night. And in an hour, it'll be in an early edition of the *Gazette.*"

He took the pages. She watched as he began reading silently, looked up at her, then scanned the rest quickly. When he finished, he took a long moment before looking at her again.

"This is really moving."

He looked at it again and began to read aloud. "*More than anything, our Christmas Star is the promise of hope. Even in my darkest hours, looking up at that star I could not help but feel it. The stories we all have of our hopes and dreams and love that surround our star are like a collective prayer. And the light that emanates from it will never go out, even if we don't get it lit. But we must.*"

He looked at her.

"Ryan, we don't have a lot of time to raise the money and then get the work done, but I wanted to ask you one more time, if we can do it, are you going to stand in our way?"

She could see his inner turmoil as he clenched his jaw as if he was trying hard not to say something. He walked to the window and looked up at the damaged star. She was getting nervous, and frustrated. Finally, he turned back to her.

"I'm sorry," he said softly.

"What? You ... you can't be serious, Ryan? I think you have some idea now what this star means to everyone. How can you just say no?"

"Look, I already told you. When I bought this place, the star was already destroyed. I'm not going to take this on, I can't."

"And I already told you that no one expects you to fix it. That would be impossible. We're gathering a crew of professionals and volunteers. As for the money, yes, it's astronomical."

But it was as if he wasn't even listening. He just stood there shaking his head. "This isn't fair."

"I don't want this to end up in court, Ryan. But if it does, you'll lose."

His eyes widened. "What are you talking about?"

"The deed restriction? If you own the property, you have to allow the star to be lit. If we can fix it, you won't have a choice."

He just stared at her, saying nothing. She turned to leave.

"Hope!"

She turned and he stood there, looking at her in disbelief.

"I know this is going to take a miracle, Ryan. But I can't give up believing in them. And this one ... this one I need."

She opened the door and left without another word.

Her feet were shaking on the brake pedal as she slid down Buck Hill Lane, which had turned icy from the melting snow. Even her hands trembled as she gripped the steering wheel. She hated confrontation, it always seemed to shatter her nerves. But she couldn't believe how stubborn Ryan was being. Something just didn't make sense. Unless the side of him that had been so kind to Zach and her dad, and even her, well, maybe that was all just an act. A way to get work, a free meal ... no, that just didn't ring true.

Then what was it?

Or maybe he was as private as he first let on. Christmas, after all, wasn't his thing. He'd had a painful childhood and the memories of his injuries and those he lost were obviously wrapped up in the holiday. But he'd never seen the star and maybe, just maybe, it would give him some kind of peace. And hope. And he could finally heal from those things.

If she was even right about that.

As she drove through town, Main Street was buzzing with shopkeepers putting last-minute decorations up. The gas lanterns were glowing, though it wasn't even noon yet, and the sky seemed to be getting even darker. She wondered if a storm was brewing. It sure looked like it.

At the intersection of Grand Avenue, she sat at the light staring up at Santa and his reindeer, hanging across the street on the wire Ryan strung and finessed to suit her, feeling as though she'd reached a difficult crossroad. And dreading what she might ultimately have to do. Remembering the Robert Frost poem from high school English, the lines came to her suddenly:

Two roads diverged in a wood, and I—I took the one less traveled by, And that has made all the difference.

Which road would she take now? Would she back down? Or will she fight? She knew there wasn't really a choice. She couldn't give up now.

Though she loathed confrontation, and from what she could see so did Ryan, there was no doubt a confrontation of major proportions was brewing. And she didn't like it one bit.

But what could she do? She knew that road was the right one. But the thought of escalating this little skirmish into a major battle was horrible. She didn't want to put either one of them through it. But what other option was there?

As the light changed, she realized where she could go for an answer. She headed straight down Main Street, stopping at Calico Country Flowers. Then she drove to the end of Main Street, veering right onto Mountain Avenue, taking her to the other side of town. Soon she turned and went through the giant stone arch and crossed over a little wooden bridge that clattered as she went over the river and into Union Cemetery.

As a girl, she sometimes played here. It had always seemed more like a park, with its big trees, small hills and winding lanes. And of course, there was the river where she'd learned to fish with her dad and where the Memorial Day Parade always concluded with poignant speeches and a float sailing down the river to the haunting bugle sounds of Taps. And now this place held a new reverence for her. She should have come sooner. But it was always so hard.

She drove the winding gravel lanes until she was in a newer section, then parked. She got out, walking across a stretch of grass, past grave markers with names that were all too familiar in this small town. Halfway down the row, she stopped in front of a heart-shaped marble stone. She pulled her gloves off and reached out, her fingers tracing the words carved into the stone: *Alice Anne McClain, Beloved Wife & Mother.* She placed the bouquet of red roses she just bought on the snow in front of the stone. Her eyes suddenly filled with tears.

"Oh, Mom," she whispered, "how I miss you!"

She took a deep breath, looking across the river at the town, the gold dome of the college in the distance, the white spire of the Presbyterian Church, and on the far side of the valley, Buck Hill.

"I want to bring the star back, Mom. I know now what it really meant to you. But I'm so afraid I'm going to let everyone down. I think I'll probably lose my job. And I have to move Zach again. I'm scared I'm failing on all fronts and ... despite everything I wrote, I'm trying so hard not to give up hope. But even if I do make it happen, there's someone who might stand in my way."

She reached out again, her fingers caressing the smooth, cold stone, wishing somehow for something more. "You always made me feel like there wasn't anything I couldn't do, Mom. If you were here ... " She shook her head, the ache in her heart so deep it hurt to breathe. Then she put her fingertips to her lips, kissed them, and brushed them against the stone one more time.

She turned and began to walk away. Halfway down the row, she stopped suddenly as a thought popped into her head. She stood there thinking for several minutes. Slowly she began to smile. "Of course," she whispered to herself.

Then she pulled her phone out of her purse, punching in a familiar number.

"Debora Redmond, Features," her boss answered.

"Hi, Debora, it's Hope."

"You'd better be calling to tell me you're sending your article now," her boss said in a clipped voice.

"Yes. No. I mean I'll have it to you shortly. I just have a

few tweaks left."

"Good, because the other three turned theirs in yesterday."

That didn't make her look so good. "Debora, I ... I didn't write what you wanted, about Christmas in the city."

"Why not? That's what the assignment was."

"Well, I was kind of stuck and ... I've got something that was really speaking to me. I think you're going to like it. I'm titling it 'Memories of Christmas Past.'"

There was a long pause. "Sounds like something out of Dickens." Her voice did not sound happy.

"It's actually something personal. About a Christmas Star that shines over the town I grew up in. Except that this year it isn't. But I think it's universal and will speak to all readers, wherever they are, about how our childhood Christmases never really leave us."

She could hear Debora sigh. "Alright, just get it to me quickly."

"Will do. Thanks."

She hung up, slipped her phone back in her purse then turned and looked at her mother's stone and blew a kiss.

"Thanks, Mom. I know that was you."

By the time she got back to her father's, Hope knew exactly how to tweak her article. She typed furiously for the next four hours and she had it done in time for an early dinner with her dad and Zach. There was no time for cookie baking, though, and she felt guilty about that. But Zach didn't seem to mind, because tonight was their big night. She would finally see the surprise they'd been working on in the garage. As soon as dinner was over, the two of them left in a hurry.

Twenty minutes later, there was a knock at the front door. She opened it and Phoebe rushed in.

"I thought we were meeting at the parade?"

"I've been texting and calling and you haven't answered!" Phoebe said.

"Sorry. I was writing and had my ringer turned off. Then we had a quick dinner."

"Oh, Hope, I couldn't wait anymore. I had to give you this before we kick off the Hometown Holiday. Your article! Everyone's talking about it."

She handed Hope a copy of the *Gazette* and there on the front page was her article.

"*The Christmas Star: Hackettstown's Beacon of Hope*" the headline began. She looked up, her eyes misting. "The last time I saw my byline in the *Gazette* was the summer before I graduated college. This feels so … " she shrugged, unable to put it into words.

"It's going to happen. I know it!" Phoebe said, practically jumping up and down. "WRNJ is doing regular updates on the star fund already."

"Really?"

"There's been a surge in donations this afternoon. Hope it's happening. Thanks to you! I told you that you could do this."

Hope's eyes widened then and Phoebe's eyebrows shot up. "What?"

She pulled Phoebe into the foyer. "We might have a problem," she whispered.

"What on earth—"

Hope put a finger to her lips. "I don't want to say anything yet."

"Come on, you're just a worrier."

"You're probably right," she said, knowing it was way more than that.

"Let's get going, everyone's waiting by the gazebo."

Just then there was another knock at the door. Hope opened it and there was Julia, in a white parka and white boots with a red scarf and hat. She looked lovely.

"Oh, Julia, perfect timing. I was about to call you to go. Somebody here is in a major hurry," she said, nodding toward Phoebe with a laugh.

"Well, it's a big night," Julia said. "And you're in for quite a surprise."

"Wait, you know?"

Julia smiled, then pretended to zip her lip.

"Okay, ladies," Phoebe said as Hope pulled on her coat and gloves. "Let's get this show on the road."

And off they went.

Walking into town everything was so beautiful that Hope felt as if she were on the set of a Christmas movie. Big snowflakes fell gently, just enough to look pretty but not cold or wet. All of the houses were lit up with twinkling white lights, or old-fashioned colored lights. There were wreaths and garlands, snowmen and blowup Santas glowing from within. Groups of people were everywhere, all heading into town, and some were even singing Christmas songs as they walked.

They headed down Main Street to the gazebo to gather with some of the others from the Hometown Holiday committee. They could already hear band music coming, meaning the parade was on its way from farther downtown. Many in the crowd were calling out to Hope that her article was going to bring the star back for sure. It was lovely to get so much affirmation, but inside a little drumbeat had begun since she'd seen the piece in print. It was all on the line now.

"Here they come!" a voice shouted.

Sure enough, the parade was approaching. The high school marching band was first in their orange and black uniforms playing a raucous version of "Jingle Bells" while the twirlers strutted, then broke into a routine that included some fancy baton tosses and dance moves. Twirling had come a long way, Hope thought, since she'd been in school.

The various bands and fire trucks and decorated cars full of dignitaries were interspersed with floats, the first of which was a long flatbed truck decked out as Santa's Workshop complete with elves making toys and one of them throwing candy canes out to children in the crowd. Then there was the Colonial Musketeers Fife and Drum Corp, a local children's band that had traveled the world, and now regaled them with "Santa Claus is Coming to Town." The next float looked like a scene from the past, as a man and woman in gorgeous Victorian garb waltzed slowly to the music of a violinist standing beside a Christmas tree decorated with lace garland and crystal balls. She was surprised when the dancing couple slowly turned to see that the woman in the beautiful mauve gown was none other than Lauren, who stopped suddenly, looking over toward them and blew a kiss. Hope's eyes followed her gesture, and there was Ryan, just a few feet behind them, who looked embarrassed. Suddenly his eyes met hers. He blushed then shrugged, as if to say … she wasn't quite sure.

"Hope look, there they are!" Julia shouted, grabbing her arm.

Hope turned around and here came her father's flatbed truck turned float. They'd added an extension onto the back of the truck and the float was now … a replica of her old bedroom with Zach sitting on the bed looking out a window to a small hill with a star on top.

"Oh … I can't believe they did this!"

"They wanted you to have your star," Julia whispered.

She was trying to keep her composure but her eyes filled with tears that she wiped away quickly and her throat ached with the effort of not crying with joy. Zach was smiling and looking out at the crowd, knowing she'd be at the gazebo.

"Zach, over here!" she called out, waving her arms.

His searching eyes found her and he gave her such a triumphant smile it nearly undid her.

As they passed, she turned to call out a thank you to Ryan. She knew her father could never have managed all that without him. But he was gone.

"Oh, Julia," she said, turning to her and giving her a hug. "How on earth did you ever keep that a secret?"

"It wasn't easy, believe me."

The parade continued for another half hour until the final float, which was always tradition: Santa Claus beside Rudolph calling out "Merry Christmas" to the crowd, who cheered endlessly.

"I think that was our best Santa Parade ever," Phoebe said.

Hope laughed, "I think you used to say that every year, but … this year I think it's really true."

"Mom! Mom!"

They all turned and there was Zach running toward them, with Red trying to keep up.

"Oh, Zach," she cried when he ran right into her arms. She hugged him fiercely. "That was the best surprise of my life!"

"It was all Zach's idea," her dad said, a bit out of breath.

She looked at her son and took his face in her hands. "That meant the world to me, Zach."

"Thanks, Mom," he said, and then grew serious. "In case you don't get the star back, I wanted you to have one. So did Grandpa and Ryan."

She looked at her dad then. "Thank you, Dad. I know it was a lot of work, and at a time when you're really busy at the store."

"Nonsense. Zach and I had a blast."

She looked around. "Has anyone seen Ryan? I'd like to thank him, too."

"There he is," Zach said, pointing toward Stella's Café where an ice sculpture was now in progress on the sidewalk. Zach took her hand and began pulling her in that direction. "Come on, Mom."

They all walked over, which took some weaving through the crowds. As they got closer, they could see a man with a chainsaw working his way artistically through a block of ice.

They stood next to Ryan, who nodded a greeting as it was impossible to talk over the noise. As the ice took shape, and shards of it flew, the crowd grew, and before they knew it, the simple block of ice had become an intricate snowman, complete with hat, scarf, mittens, and a corn cob pipe to boot.

"Just like Frosty," Zach said after the crowd applauded.

"Exactly," she said, smiling.

"Ryan, Mom loved the float," Zach said then, giving Ryan a high five.

"I'm glad, Buddy," Ryan said, glancing at her.

"I came over to say thank you, Ryan," she said, her tone a bit frosty, too. "For helping with the float. You were right, I was very surprised."

Her dad cleared his throat. "Honey, how about we take Zach for some cocoa to warm up. You can catch up with us."

She nodded and watched for a moment as they walked up the street. Then she turned back to Ryan.

"I'm glad you liked it, Hope."

"I just … I don't understand you. One minute you're all not into Christmas, and then you do something so thoughtful. And now you know this whole town wants to see the star lit again and … you don't even care!"

"I never said I didn't care."

Her jaw dropped. "Seriously? How can you expect me to believe—"

"Ryan!"

Her words were cut off and they both turned to see Lauren coming in her beautiful mauve Victorian gown with crystal snowflakes shimmering in her hair. She looked stunning. Ryan just stared at her, speechless.

"Ryan, our angel is slipping from the wire across Church Street. Would you mind seeing if you can do something quickly?"

"Sure. Would you excuse me, Hope?"

Lauren turned to her then, as if in surprise. "Oh, Hope, I'm sorry, I didn't see you there."

"I was just leaving." She turned away, though she was simmering inside, wanting to finish the conversation with Ryan. She nearly bumped into Phoebe's parents.

"Oh, Hope, your article was just beautiful," Mrs. Hodge said, giving her a quick hug.

"Great job, Hope," Mr. Hodge added with a smile.

"You know all Phoebe can talk about is how wonderful it is that you're back. You two girls were such good friends. I think she's missed that."

"Well, I'll be leaving soon, but we'll stay in touch, I promise."

She nodded and they began to walk away. As she turned to find her dad and Zach, she realized something and rushed back to the Hodge.

"Mr. Hodge," she called out and they both turned.

"Yes, Hope, what can I do for you?"

"I was wondering if I could call you tomorrow. I have a possible legal issue I'd like to talk to you about."

"Of course, but I'll be leaving first thing in the morning for some depositions out of town for a few days. Can we talk on Thursday?"

"Yes, of course. Thank you so much."

By the time she found her dad and Julia in front of Marley's Grill, where the hot chocolate station was set up, she could see Zach was fading.

"I think it's time we get you home to bed, young man. You've had quite a day."

"He sure did," her dad said, patting him on the head.

"And we've got some lessons first thing in the morning, now that your calendar has cleared up," Julia joked.

"I can't thank you enough for that, Julia," she said fondly.

"It's truly my pleasure, Hope."

As they walked back, she noticed that her father took Julia's hand and secured it through his arm. For a moment she pictured her mother there, as they walked back from the Santa Parade year after year. And for a moment, her heart squeezed with sadness. But then she looked at her son, smiling and skipping, despite being so tired. And there in that smile, for the first time, she saw his resemblance to her mother.

CHAPTER 12

TWO DAYS AFTER THE SANTA Parade, Hope walked into the kitchen to find her dad, Julia and Zach at the table eating sandwiches. The radio was on and they were listening to Christmas music. She grabbed a cookie from the counter.

"Honey, sit down and eat a sandwich with us," her dad said.

"Dad, I can't. I'm trying to finish up the attic before we leave."

Just then the music ended.

"Oh, listen up, everyone," Julia said quickly. "I think they're about to give another update on the star fund."

Her dad got up and raised the volume.

"On this merry December 15th," the radio DJ began, "I am pleased to announce that our Christmas Star fund is ... getting closer to our goal! Open up your wallets, folks. 'Tis the season!"

She stood there, her heart sinking, as her father turned the radio off.

"Hope, don't look so worried," Julia said.

"They're not announcing numbers because we still have

so far to go. They've been saying the same thing since yesterday afternoon. It's like after that first flurry of donations, it's gotten quiet."

"Have faith," her dad said.

"Mr. Durling has the power company lined up for the 20th, to fix the main lines running up Buck Hill. That gives us four days left to raise thousands still."

Her dad got up and came over to her and put his hands on her shoulders. "Listen, if we get closer, I'll donate the rest. I'm not going to let you be disappointed. Or Zach."

"You will not, Dad! I know you already made quite a large contribution. And you're trying to retire! And move!"

Her dad looked over at Julia who shook her head.

"See even Julia agrees that's crazy. Now, I'm nearly done with the attic. You guys finish your lunch and then Zach, I want you to complete that last assignment, okay?"

"Yes, Mom."

"He's nearly finished. Don't worry," Julia assured her.

"Okay then," she said, grabbing another cookie and heading back upstairs. "If all goes well, I could be finished with the attic today."

She was amazed at how much she'd accomplished in the past few days since she began to put all of her energy back into the attic. In between Christmas events, that was. The boxes were piling up and there were a number of plastic bins her father had brought home that held things either he, or she, would keep. She turned music on her phone and sang along to Christmas carols as she worked, trying hard to stay hopeful. Hours later, she was taping a box closed when the music stopped suddenly as her cell began to ring. When she saw who it was, she tossed the tape aside and picked right up.

"Oh, hi Mr. Hodge. I've been hoping to hear back from you. And I can't thank you enough for checking into this for me." She stood there listening, her eyes growing wider. Her heart sinking. "You're absolutely certain of that?"

"I'm sorry, Hope. I am."

"I just ... I can't believe it. I guess no one ever had to look into this before because ... there was never a need to?"

"I think you're right, dear."

"Mr. Hodge, can we just keep this between us for now, please?"

"Of course. And Hope, I'm sorry."

"Thank you."

She hung up and stood there, her heart racing. She knew now what it meant when someone said their blood was boiling. She felt as if she might explode.

"Ryan Miller! How could you!" she shouted in the empty attic.

And then she stormed down the stairs.

It was nearly dark and still snowing gently when she drove up Buck Hill, parking beside the workshop. Ryan was outside, his arms full of boards he was apparently moving from the pile. He turned at the sound of her car and put the wood down. He walked over, Kodi following at his heels.

She got out and before he could say a word, she exploded. "How could you not tell me?"

He closed his eyes, shaking his head with a loud sigh.

"How could you let me write the article, start the star fund, knowing all along that … you'd never let it happen. And that there was nothing I could do about it."

She waited, hands on her hips, trying to slow her breathing. His face hardened then. He was obviously upset. Kodi whined and began nudging his leg.

"Oh, wait," she continued since he was obviously not going to respond, "you never said a word because you thought I couldn't actually make it happen!"

"That is not true!" he finally shouted.

"Then tell me what is. Because all this time I thought there was a clause in the deed here that whoever owns the property has to allow the star. My dad and everyone else assumed this, too, because there was never any reason to think otherwise. But … it turns out it wasn't in the deed. It was just a 'gentleman's agreement.' And every person who has owned this land since Doc Stevens first put up the star has honored it. Until you, Ryan."

He looked up at the treetops, shaking his head, then turned away from her. Suddenly he turned back. "I never signed on for this, Hope. I've just been trying to live my life in peace up here."

"So you had no idea when you bought this property?"

"It was mentioned by my attorney, right before I closed. He was also surprised it wasn't in the deed. I told him I wouldn't close if I couldn't eventually take it down."

"And you never thought twice, watching me and the entire town getting excited and … hopeful about bringing this piece of history back?"

He didn't answer.

"Ryan!"

"I thought I could—" he shouted then abruptly stopped.

"You thought you could what?"

His face reddened and she could see he was trying hard not to speak as he now stared up at the damaged star. Kodi continued to whimper.

"Ryan, what are you not saying?"

He looked at her then as he reached down and stroked Kodi's head to calm him. "You can have your star, Hope. Just not this year."

"What do you mean?"

"I realized these past few weeks that it's time for me to move on. I'll be selling this place."

"But ... that makes no sense. You said this was becoming home. You were—"

He put a hand up stopping her. "I've never stayed any place for very long. I prefer it that way. I'll put it in the deed when I sell, so you'll never have to worry again. You'll have your star next year."

She stared at him in disbelief. He turned then back to the boards he'd dropped when she arrived.

"What about your business? Your workshop expansion?"

"I'll sell the lumber. That's not a problem," he said, picking up a stack of boards.

"Ryan," she said and he turned and looked at her. "You told me that you thought I always tried to see the best in people. You're right. I did that with you and ... once again I was wrong."

She turned, got in her car and pulled out of the driveway.

When she was gone, he dropped the wood and stood there, catching his breath as if he'd run a mile. It was true, he'd never signed up for this. All he wanted was to live up here in peace, despite the friendly townspeople who kept trying to draw him in. But then Hope walked into his life, with those wide gray eyes and that heart of hers that had to fix everything and everyone. And to see her look at him as she just did, with disappointment and hurt … it felt as though he'd been punched in the chest.

It wasn't just her, though. Now everyone would know the truth, including Zach. He thought of that first morning the little boy came all the way up the mountain, trying to find out how to make his mother happy again. What would he think of Ryan now? He knew the boy looked up to him. And he knew he was partly responsible for the change in Zach, from serious worrier to happy and excited.

Then there was Red. He admired Red McClain so much. He wasn't just the kind of father anyone would be happy to have. He was a man of honor and pride. Red had begun mentoring him from the get-go, though they'd never talked about anything personal. Sometimes men didn't have to.

How could he possibly stay here after letting all of them down? It had come to him at that moment that she was shouting at him, and he'd realized in that instant, yes, he would leave. And she could have her star back. So would the town.

But where would he go this time? Starting over once more filled him with dread.

He walked over to the star with Kodi again at his heels. He looked up at the damaged structure, all twisted metal and broken glass and dangling wires, the cause of all his fears and misery. Suddenly he began punching it, slamming the base over and over with his fist until it began to bleed. He couldn't stop. Kodi was barking furiously as he circled him in panic. Finally spent, Ryan sank to the ground, shaking his head, chest heaving for air, pulling the dog into his arms to calm him.

CHAPTER 13

HOPE WAS STILL SHAKING AS she pulled down her dad's street. Then she saw them, her son and her father, putting the finishing touches on a snowman. She pulled over, not wanting to turn in the drive and interrupt their fun. Her dad was straightening the snowman's head as Zach ran into the house and came out a moment later with his arms full. She watched as they put a hat and scarf on their creation and then finished with black button eyes and a carrot stick for a nose. They high-fived and then her dad pulled Zach into a long hug. Her eyes filled with tears she quickly wiped away. Then she pulled into the driveway with a little honk and they turned, Zach calling out to her excitedly.

"Wow, that is some snowman!" she exclaimed, as she got out of the car.

"Zach got inspired by the ice sculpture the other night," her dad said, smiling.

"I'm sorry, Honey. I know I promised I'd make one with you."

"It's okay, Mom, I know you've been busy. But can you

take a picture of me and Grandpa with the snowman so I can show Dad?"

"Sure thing."

She took out her cell and they posed over and over, peeking from behind, making believe they were shaking hands, having a conversation with Frosty, just cracking themselves up. It made her so sad to have to burst this bubble. But really, she had no choice.

"How about we go inside and I'll make some hot chocolate for you guys to warm up."

"Yay!" Zach shouted as they all went inside.

She waited until they were all seated at the island. "Listen, guys, you know the old 'I've got some good news, and some bad news' saying?'"

They both looked at her and nodded.

"Well, I've got some bad news, and some good news."

"What is it, Hope?" her dad said, looking worried.

"There's not going to be a star this year."

"But Mom, you can't give up!" Zach pleaded.

"Honey, please believe me, it just can't be helped. And it's okay," she said, trying to smile. "Because we tried, and that's what counts. I want you to always remember that."

He came over and gave her a hug. "I will. I'm sorry, Mom."

"Hey are you kidding?" she said, pulling him apart so she could look into his eyes. "Your amazing float had my star and that meant more to me than anything."

"Thanks, Mom. But if that's the bad news, then what's the good news?"

"Well, there's a chance there might be a star next year."

It sounded lame. Like when she'd tell him "We'll see" about something he wanted, but it really meant no.

"Then there's hope," her dad chimed in.

"Yes," she said. "Now, Zach, I want you to go put some dry clothes on so we can go on our horse and carriage ride through town tonight. It's our last night."

"I know, Mom," Zach said a little forlornly.

"Hey, we stayed way longer than we planned and it's time we head home. You've got a big trip to get ready for and I've got more packing to do there."

Zach ran upstairs and she began cleaning up. Her dad came over and pulled her into a hug.

"I don't know what I was thinking, Dad. How could I have gotten so caught up in everything here? I lost sight of what I really should have been focused on."

"Honey, what happened?"

"Ryan won't allow the star to be fixed, even if we raise the money. And I thought there was a clause in the deed about the star. That whoever owned the land had to allow it to be lit. But there's not."

"Are you sure? I always thought that was the case, too."

She nodded. "All these years it's just been a gentleman's agreement. Mr. Hodge researched it for me."

"I can't believe it."

"I know. And I guess there was never a reason to look into it. Until now."

"I'm just surprised about Ryan," her dad said.

"Actually, I'm not."

Her father just stood there, shaking his head with

disappointment.

"Hey, Dad, it's okay. It's been an amazing time here. And I'm so glad Zach got to do so many wonderful Christmas things. I have you to thank for most of that."

He pulled her into another hug. "I loved every moment of it. And having you here."

"Then please don't be upset about this. We have to be thankful for what we did have."

"That we do, yes."

She went upstairs then to get ready for their last night in town.

Something wasn't right. Red knew it in his bones. It didn't take him long, when he'd first met Ryan, to know the kind of man he was. A good, and honorable, man. One who didn't share a lot, but Red knew that didn't mean he wasn't feeling it inside. He reminded him so much of himself.

That Ryan was letting this happen this way just didn't make sense. He saw how he looked at Hope. In those unguarded moments, that wasn't difficult to see. And the way he'd been with Zach! Red couldn't have asked for a better role model.

Why would Ryan willingly let Hope and Zach both be hurt by refusing to let the star be fixed?

After the superstorm, when the star was damaged so badly, he'd sort of made peace with the fact that it was no doubt gone for good. After all, everything else of importance had disappeared from his life. First Alice. And then Hope. But since she returned and reignited that long-forgotten dream of getting the star up and shining again, Red didn't just want it to happen, he needed it to happen. Hope was back, things had healed between them. And it was part of their legacy. It was part of Alice. He probably couldn't explain it to someone if he tried. But somehow, to make everything right, back to the way it was supposed to be, the star had to shine again.

Looking out the kitchen window to the darkness at the top of Buck Hill, he could remember carrying the wooden pieces of the star up that mountain each Christmas of his boyhood. The star would be erected and finally they'd watch it light up the first of December and each night thereafter through the entire Christmas season. Then they would take it apart and carry the wooden pieces back down again. Those trips up and down, trudging through the snow, were sometimes so brutally cold, he couldn't feel his toes through his boots. One year he even caught pneumonia and worried the next he wouldn't be allowed to participate. But he was one of the regular group of men and boys who carried out what was deemed a sacred mission in this town year after year. Until that permanent star was finally erected.

Just then he heard the door close upstairs. They were coming down now to go to their last night at the Hometown Holiday. He'd have to make up an excuse because he was supposed to be going with them. But he couldn't.

He had to go talk to Ryan and somehow make this right. The star had to be lit. It had to shine again this Christmas.

While Zach finished getting bundled up, Hope came down

and found her father in his recliner in the family room.

"Dad, I thought you were getting ready to go with us?"

"Honey, I think I'm going to take a little snooze. It's been a long day."

"Oh, Dad, I'm sorry if we've worn you out."

"Nonsense, I've been having a great time. Maybe I'll meet you there later. Now you two go and have a good time."

"Are you sure? I mean we could stay home."

"No. You and Zach go enjoy."

"Okay. And I'm glad you're listening to your body and taking it easy. I know Zach can be a handful."

Her dad laughed. "He makes me feel young again."

Just then Zach bounded down the stairs. "I'm ready."

"Okay, then. Off we go," she said, handing him his coat.

They headed into town, holding hands as they walked, which Hope was surprised again that Zach let her do. But he was so busy talking a mile a minute about the evening ahead. When they got to Main Street, they wove through the crowded sidewalks, where people were pausing to admire all of the ice sculptures, now finished in front of many of the shops. Zach's favorite was the wooden soldier, which was about six feet tall and standing at attention. They stopped again at Stella's Café, where the servers were handing out gingerbread men, fresh and warm from the oven and decorated with delicious white icing. Then they went to the gazebo for the countdown of the tree lighting. It was one of her favorite things. As the high school chorus sang "Oh Christmas Tree," everyone joined in. Soon it was time for the big moment. Even Zach counted down along with the crowd, "Five, four, three, two, one!" His face lit up even brighter than the tree when the thirty-foot-tall blue spruce was suddenly illuminated.

"Wow, Mom, that's the biggest tree I ever saw," he said excitedly. "Next to the one we decorated at Grandpa's," he quickly added.

"Come on," she said before the crowd dispersed. "It looks like the line is going down for the carriage rides."

They hurried over to the firehouse on Moore Street, just a half block away, and got in line. Madrigal singers in Victorian costume sang old Christmas hymns, their beautiful harmonies entertaining those waiting for their turns. Soon they heard the clip-clop of horse hooves coming closer and a minute later an antique carriage draped with white lights stopped in front of them. Hope and Zach climbed up and sat on leather benches with a handful of others, snuggling close to stay warm. And then with a snap of the reins, the carriage took off, pulled by a beautiful white horse, as big as a Clydesdale, adorned with bells. As they headed toward the historic college section, the air was filled with the sound of the jingling bells and hooves clip-clopping on the pavement.

They passed old Victorians with gingerbread trim, turrets and wrap-around porches covered in Christmas lights. One had a replica of the sleigh they were on, filled with colorfully wrapped presents. Craftsman houses interspersed the Victorians, with window boxes full of holly and eaves dripping icicle lights, their front lawns filled with assorted decorations. Christmas music was playing from many of the porches, from Mannheim Steamroller to Bing Crosby. It was all breathtaking.

"Mom, it's so beautiful here," Zach said, looking up at her

with an awestruck smile.

"I know, Zach."

And it was true. No one did Christmas, in her experience, quite like this town.

Later that night, when Zach was fast asleep, Hope went downstairs and began tucking presents under the tree. Her phone dinged, and when she reached for it, her eyes widened in surprise. It was Debora Redmond, her editor. Oh ... this was it. The decision. Her heart began to beat like a trip hammer. She knew she really didn't deserve to keep this job and it was her own fault. She hadn't even handed in what she'd been assigned to write. But she'd put all of her heart into the article about the star, which looked like it would be for nothing.

Taking a deep breath, she swiped to open the message: *Dear Hope, While it's always difficult to tell someone they are out of a job right before Christmas ...*

Oh, no. She couldn't continue reading. She put the phone down and walked across the room, pacing and trying to calm down. What a fool she'd been, throwing away her future, and Zach's, for a dream that never could have happened, because of Ryan. And he didn't even have the guts to tell her the truth. She'd risked everything. And now ...

Sighing, she picked up the phone and swiped it open again to read the rest of Debora's message and face the music. As she began reading, her mouth fell open and she began to laugh out loud. *But I'm happy to inform you that the* Tribune *would like you to stay on as a Senior Features Writer.*

"Oh my God!" she squealed out loud, hugging the phone to her chest. This was unbelievable! *While your article about the star in your hometown was not quite what we had in mind, it showcased your beautiful writing and ability to tug at heartstrings, even with a humbug like me. We'll be running it in a special Christmas supplement on Christmas Eve. Congratulations! Debora.*

Just then she heard the front door close and a moment later her father came into the room.

"Dad, where have you been? I thought you'd gone up to bed while we were out. You said you were tired."

"I went to see Ryan."

"Oh, Dad, I wish you hadn't."

He unzipped his coat and tossed it on the couch. Then he came over to her and took her hand. "I couldn't just let it go. I could see how upset you were."

"I'm okay, Dad. I was more upset for Zach."

"Come and sit down," he said, leading her to the sofa, where he sat down.

Hope sat on the coffee table, facing him.

"Honey, it just didn't make sense to me that Ryan would break a 'gentleman's agreement.' He's a Marine, after all, just like my father, and I know that in or out of uniform, they live their lives bound by a code of honor and service. So for him to do this … I knew there had to be a damn good reason for him to break it."

"I honestly can't imagine what that would be. Knowing that an entire town had pinned its hopes on that star being lit again. It wasn't just me."

"Hope, vets don't usually talk about their service. Or their scars. Except maybe to other vets. I also saw that with my dad. It took me some time, but I finally got Ryan to open up to me. And he'll probably get mad at me for sharing this with you, but I think I have to. I think you need to know the truth."

"Dad, he told me about his leg injury."

"I'm not talking about something physical, Honey."

"Oh?"

Her dad sighed, and she could see he was trying to choose his words carefully.

"You can't think less of Ryan because he doesn't want the star fixed, or lit. Believe it or not, he actually was trying to let it happen. He wanted to. He thought he could. But ... then he started getting flashbacks."

"Flashbacks? What do you mean?"

"Ryan still has some emotional trauma from that explosion in Iraq that wounded his leg and killed his buddies. I don't think he told you, but he also had a bad head injury and now ... certain bright or sudden harsh lights can be a trigger for him."

"PTSD?"

Her dad nodded. And she sat there trying to process it all.

"So the star might be a trigger if it were lit?"

He nodded. "Hope, imagine the star all lit up, hundreds of lights shining there right above his house, every time he opened the door and went outside. Or lighting up suddenly when he walked out of his workshop. The thought of it was traumatic for him."

She sat there, imagining it. The lights of her beloved star triggering a moment of fear and chaos and death for him. Right there above his own home. *I just wanted to live my life in peace here,* he told her earlier that day. What he had seen, and suffered, she could only imagine.

"Oh, Dad, I feel so horrible. The things I said to him. He was so nonchalant about his leg, I had no idea there was more to it. I was so angry with him! And I said such terrible things!"

"Hope, there's no way you could have known about this. You know there was one time a light bulb blew in the attic, when he first came to look at the job up there, and he got really jumpy. I should have realized something then, but he covered it up pretty quickly. I imagine he's probably gotten pretty good at that so no one would pick up on it."

She jumped up. "Dad, I need to go apologize to him."

"Honey, no," her dad said, taking her arm to hold her there. "You have to give it time. It wasn't easy for him to talk about. And he … he feels just awful. Hope, he cares about you. A great deal."

Her eyes filled with tears. She walked over to the tree and stood there, picturing him there decorating it with her and Zach. How he seemed to let go for a while and even enjoy himself. But then she remembered that when they lit the tree with such excitement, she'd thought it odd that he'd been looking down at the floor at first. Not looking at the sudden lighting of the tree, the big moment of fanfare. And now she knew why. He'd been avoiding the illumination. That sudden intense moment of bright light.

She went and sat back down again, looking at her father. "Dad, I care about him, too. I was starting to even think … " she couldn't finish.

"Think what?"

"You know what? It doesn't matter. We're leaving tomorrow anyway. It's fine. Zach is my priority and I've got to quickly find us another house."

"Hope."

"Don't worry about me, please." She stood then. "My friend Lily is looking for us and I'm sure she'll find us something. And there is some good news, Dad. I just found out that I'm keeping my job with the *Tribune*. In fact, I even have a new title, Senior Features Writer. So now I can find us something permanent."

Her dad seemed stunned.

"Congratulations, Hope," he said, after a pause. "That is good news."

"Thanks. I love you, Dad." She got up and kissed his forehead. "I'm going to get to bed now. It's late and we've got an early start tomorrow."

"I love you, too, Honey. Good night."

She went upstairs. Red sat for a long time, staring at the Christmas tree. He should have been happy for his daughter, keeping the job she'd been so worried about. Being appreciated for her writing. But all he could think about was tomorrow after her car pulled away. And how lonely he was going to be once again.

The next morning, they were all in the foyer putting on coats, Hope and Zach's suitcases already in the car, along with the boxes she was taking back with her. Hope watched as Julia hugged Zach and he promised to keep up with all of his school-work. Then Zach turned and hugged her dad, long and hard, and Hope felt her throat swell with emotion. Just as her dad turned to her, there was a knock at the door. Her dad opened the door and there was Ryan with his toolbox. He stood there as an awkward silence grew.

"Ryan, I'm going to Hawaii with my dad for Christmas," Zach said then. "He's gonna teach me how to surf."

"That's really great, Zach. I hope you have a Merry Christmas." He looked over at her then, clearly uncomfortable. "And you, too, Hope."

Words failed her. And then her dad took Zach by the hand.

"Come on, Buddy, I'll get you buckled in."

They left and Julia followed, closing the door quickly, leaving her and Ryan standing there in silence.

"Ryan, I'm so sorry, I never should have—"

"It's fine," he interrupted, "no worries. I know you've got a long drive and I'm planning to finish up with the attic today, so … safe travels."

She was startled by his cool tone. She searched his eyes, but they were looking down at the floor. She nodded, finally. "Thank you. Merry Christmas."

She picked up her purse, opened the door, and left. For a long moment, she stood on the porch, sick at heart. Then she put on a smile, walked over to the car and hugged her dad and Julia. Finally, she closed Zach's door, got in, and they waved and backed down the driveway. When she was on the street, she looked up to see Ryan in the attic window, looking down at her.

CHAPTER 14

LUCKILY, EVEN AFTER HOPE'S EXTENDED vacation, Debora was in the holiday spirit and agreed to some half days so she could get some packing done while Zach was still at school. She and Debora had always had a rather formal work relationship, but something in her boss seemed to have relaxed in the time Hope was gone. Plus, it was Christmas, and though she'd missed the holiday party, there was still a festive and loose atmosphere at work.

Each day when she got home, the "Under Contract" sign on the front lawn made Hope's heart sink. Although she was packing, she still had no idea where they were going. She was hoping desperately they wouldn't end up in a garden apartment. Having a house with a yard, and not being attached to noisy neighbors, or nasty ones, was paramount. She didn't want to bring Zach back into that again.

Late on Saturday morning, Hope was carrying a box from her bedroom and stacking it in the living room corner when she overheard Zach telling Jackson, Lily's nephew, about his sleigh -riding adventure as they played a video game on the floor.

"I've never seen snow," Jackson said in his southern lilt.

"It's really cool," Zach said. "We made a snowman, too."

"Yeah, but we've got the beach. And you don't have to be cold to have fun."

"It's not really cold, not if you dress right," Zach said.

Hope walked over before this progressed. They were best friends, but sometimes their competitive natures won out.

"You guys getting hungry?" she asked.

"Can we have mac and cheese?" Zach asked.

"I like mac and cheese," Jackson piped in politely.

"Sure thing," she said, smiling. "Give me a few minutes and I'll get it started."

As she headed back into the bedroom, to empty another drawer of summer clothes, which she wouldn't be needing for months, she heard them talking about their favorite foods and laughed. Sometimes a little distraction was all it took to keep the peace. A few minutes later, there was a knock on the open bedroom door and she looked up to see Lily.

"Oh, I didn't hear you come in."

"I don't think the boys did, either. They were hot and heavy into a video game."

"I just offered the boys lunch, if that's okay. I didn't think you had any plans for Jackson, did you?"

"Not a one. His mom is Christmas shopping and I'm tied up with paperwork, so I appreciate it."

"Good."

"But I did actually come over to tell you that I've got some good news."

"A new listing?" she asked excitedly.

201

"Yes, it's coming on just after the new year and it's in your price range and only about a half mile from here. It's vacant, so you can probably move right in. Best of all, Zach wouldn't have to change schools."

"Oh, Lil, tell me it has a nice yard?"

"Well, it is a condo, so no yard, really, just a patio. But there's a big playground nearby."

She sighed, sitting on the edge of the bed. "I really want a yard for Zach, Lil. I know I'm being picky and shouldn't be …"

"Listen, it's going to be okay. I promise we will find something."

"But time is racing by. I'm starting to get nervous."

"Let me put more feelers out in my office, see what everyone's got coming on the market after the new year. And if I have to, I will go door to door!"

She got up and gave her friend a hug. "I love you."

"I love you, too. And now I want to ask you, no I'm telling you, you are coming to my house for Christmas dinner while Zach is away. My whole family will be there. It'll be fun."

"And that cousin you've been trying to fix me up with won't be there?"

"Promise."

"I don't know, Lil. I appreciate the offer. Zach keeps pushing me to go back to my Dad's after he leaves with Drew. But … I just can't. Not after everything that happened."

"You mean with Ryan?"

She nodded. "It's so hard to explain, Lil. I mean, I feel horrible and guilty about his PTSD from Iraq. And then, when

I think about the star and everything I went through, I feel betrayed. And I know I shouldn't, but ... " She shrugged.

"Whoever said emotions were supposed to make sense? Of course, yours are all over the place. The trip back home alone was like a minefield for you, what with your dad and everything you told me about your mom."

"I know. I've got a major case of guilt there, too. I never should have stayed away so long."

"Look, from what you told me, your dad had a bit to do with that. Two stubborn people make it tough to find common ground, but you did, right?"

"We did. And I think we're in a good place now. He calls Zach every single night and they talk and talk. It's so wonderful. You know Zach hasn't really had a good male role model, not with Drew anyway."

"I know that, Honey, you don't have to remind me."

"I'm really hoping that this trip to Hawaii changes some of that. We'll see."

Just then her cell rang and she picked it up, glancing at the screen. "Well speak of the devil," she whispered to Lily before pressing receive. "Hello, Drew."

"Hey, Hope, listen things have gotten a little bit complicated and—"

"Don't do this Drew," she quickly interrupted. "Not again. Not for Christmas." She could see Lily's eyes widen as she listened. And she pictured Drew in an airport because she could hear the announcements in the background.

"Hope, relax! I'm not canceling," he said in that irritatingly superior voice he used to try to steamroll her. "It's just a ...

change of plans. I'll come and get him for New Year's."

She couldn't even speak she was so floored by his nonchalance at disappointing Zach yet again. Canceling Christmas with his own son.

"Tell me Drew, what's more important this time?"

He was silent, and then she heard a woman whispering. His girlfriend, of course.

"You know what, Drew, you don't deserve him," she said, hanging up on him.

She sank to the bed, shaking.

"Oh, Hope, I am so sorry."

"I cannot believe this. And yet, why am I surprised? He's supposed to be picking Zach up in two days and now he's not." She took a deep breath. "Oh, Lil, I need to talk to Zach. He's going to be devastated."

"I'll bring Jackson home for lunch."

"I promised them mac and cheese."

"I'll make the mac and cheese. You can send Zach over after you talk. I'll take them to Dairy Queen after, tell him that."

"That's sweet. I don't think ice cream is going to soothe this, though."

They walked back to the living room to find the boys still lying on the floor with their remotes.

"Jackson, we need to head back home, Honey. I'm going to make the mac and cheese since Hope's busy packing."

"Can't Zach come with us? We're in the middle of a game," Jackson said.

"He'll be over in just a bit," Hope told them. "I need to talk to him about something first."

Zach sat up and watched Jackson leave with Lily. Then he looked at her and it was there in his eyes, the knowing, and the disappointment. Which Drew would never see. She would have given anything not to have to say the words that would come next.

She sat on the couch and patted next to her. He came and sat beside her, and she could see how hard he was fighting tears.

"It's Dad, isn't it? He's not coming."

"I'm sorry, Honey. He said he would come and get you for New Year's."

"Are we still going to Hawaii?"

"I don't know. He didn't say. I'm so sorry, Zach."

Big tears began to slip down her son's face then. She tried to pull him into a hug, but he pushed her away.

"I hate him," he whispered, then ran to his room.

She sat there with her head in her hands.

Red McClain couldn't sleep. Three days after Hope had gone with Zach, his heart was still aching. How he missed them! And Zach, his grandson. Once again Red marveled at what a joy it had been to see him go from the quiet, serious little boy who first arrived, to the one who lit up with laughter at his jokes and riddles. Who seemed to burst with excitement at simple things like Christmas cookies and snow.

And once again he thought about how much Zach needed a father figure. Red remembered himself at that age, and how he'd followed his dad around like a puppy, learning how to hike and camp, how to work at the store, and even sell trees, something he'd loved from the time he was Zach's age. And now he'd been able to do that with Zach, who learned about each variety of tree like a pro, and proudly described each type to prospective buyers. But now Zach was gone. And if he couldn't be the father figure his grandson needed, then Hope would need to find one. But his daughter had worked hard trying to prove she could do it all. To prove she was capable, independent, and didn't need Drew. But didn't she deserve a partner in life? Someone to lean on? To share life's burdens, and joys?

He sighed, his heart heavy. How could he ever leave this earth with their lives still so unsettled? Not that he was planning to go anytime soon. And the cardiologist was pleased with his blood pressure now. But that had been Alice's biggest agony—leaving Hope, in college with no mother to guide her through the most important decisions of her life to come. He remembered that day, after Hope had gone back to school, and Alice insisting it was too soon to tell her what was coming. Protecting her daughter from the impending hurt and grief for as long as possible. His Alice, so strong and capable, just like their daughter, had broken down that night.

How do I leave her, Red? My little girl?

And then Hope had surprised them, arriving for her next visit with Drew. Alice had been excited to meet him, hoping she could leave this earth with the knowledge her daughter had found someone who would cherish and care for her as she'd always been. Drew regaled them with his tales of travel and adventure. Five years older than Hope, he'd already joined the family business and bragged about his accomplishments and the security he could offer Hope. After they left, Alice had been quiet for a long, long time. It was in bed that night, by his side in the dark, that she finally spoke.

It's what he didn't say that worries me, Red. He didn't seem to take Hope's writing seriously. And he doesn't seem to have any interest in children. I don't think he's right for her, my darling. She's going to end up bending herself to fit his ideal life. His big dreams. But what about hers?

Though he'd worried about the same things, he'd hoped with time his daughter would see through the glamour and realize those same things. But Alice didn't have that time.

Red, you have to make sure she doesn't marry him. Please.

He'd promised. And it had cost him.

Now he sat in the family room, lit only by the Christmas tree they'd decorated for him. The room was in shadow, the house so quiet. He imagined all of the Christmases the three of them had shared, right here, all of the trees, all of the Christmas mornings. Alice would always come down first and get everything ready. She'd have him stationed at the foot of the stairs with a camera, and then later on, with the camcorder, to capture Hope's face as she toddled down with shrieks of excitement as she saw the presents under the tree. And then over the years, getting bigger, a teenager, then a coed. And now she was a single mother who lived twelve hours away. How he'd hoped that they could have one more Christmas together here.

But they were back in South Carolina, about to move again and not even knowing where. He could almost hear Alice whispering in the stillness: *They need us, Red.*

But now, there was only him.

Zach sulked in his room for the rest of the day. He even skipped going next door for lunch and more play time with Jackson. She kept packing, and each time she checked on him, opening the door to find him lying on his bed with a video game, he said nothing.

She even broke one of her rules and offered to have dinner in front of the TV while they watched the "The Polar Express," but he still said next to nothing. Afterwards she cleaned up while he got ready for bed, wishing there was some way she could fix this.

He was already in his PJs and in bed reading when she went in to say good night. She sat on the edge of the bed and he looked up, without smiling.

"Just a few days until Christmas," she said with probably a bit too much cheer.

He nodded.

"You know, Honey, we can still have a nice Christmas. We can even have dinner with Jackson and everyone at Lily's next door if you'd like. You guys could play together with your new presents."

He just stared at the wall, saying nothing.

"Zach, look at me please."

He turned to her. She could see the pain in his eyes and it was like a knife in her heart. She took both of his hands, squeezing them. "Listen, Zach, I am so sorry things didn't work out with your dad. And if there was anything I could do to change that you know I would. But I don't want you to—"

"I knew he wouldn't come," he said, finally breaking his hours-long silence. "He's not even sad when I leave. He doesn't even miss me."

"Oh, Zach, I'm sure that's not—"

"Grandpa misses me!" he said, now looking at her, his eyes filled with hurt. "He was sad when we left there. And yesterday when he called, he still sounded sad."

She brushed his hair from his forehead like she did when he was little and loved it, as her mind began to race.

"I told all the kids at school I was going to Hawaii and I was gonna learn how to surf. Now they're all gonna make fun of me and think I was lying. Maybe moving to a different school might not be so bad."

So that had been on his mind, after all. Moving, changing schools. Never letting on he was worried. He'd never said a word to her about it. She felt heartsick and suddenly her mind began to race.

"Listen, I have an idea. Would you like to go back to Hackettstown and spend Christmas with Grandpa?"

His eyes widened and he sat up. "Really, Mom? But what about packing for moving and everything?"

"You know what? I think we can make it work. We can get everything for the trip ready tomorrow and then … we'll leave early Christmas Eve morning."

"Really?" he asked, his excitement growing.

"I mean we'll have to come home right after Christmas but … how does that sound?"

He nodded. And then he actually smiled. She leaned over and pulled him into a tight hug.

"Mom, you're crushing me," he laughed, trying to pull away.

She let him go, laughing. "You're still my little snuggle bunny, so don't you forget it."

She hadn't called him that in years. And surprisingly, he didn't protest.

"Grandpa's gonna be so surprised! Can we go sleigh riding again, too?"

She felt lighthearted, suddenly, at his change in demeanor. "Absolutely, whatever you want."

"You don't mind all that driving, again, Mom?"

"Not at all. Honestly, I can't wait to see your grandfather's face."

"Mom! Now you can go to the Jingle Ball on Christmas Eve, just like your mom always did."

"Oh, that's okay, Honey. I think I'll just spend Christmas Eve with my favorite guy. Now you'd better get right to sleep. We've got a lot to do tomorrow."

She kissed him goodnight and got up. As she was closing his bedroom door, Zach called out to her. "Mom, wait!"

She turned. Zach was sitting up again, just visible with the night light on. "Thanks, Mom. I love you."

It took a moment before she could speak without crying. Finally, she said, "And I love you to the moon and back."

She stayed up until nearly midnight, continuing to pack and making lists as she thought of things for the trip. In forty-eight hours, they would be back in Hackettstown. The thought was overwhelming. She'd already emailed Debora and took her last 2 sick days for the year, which she'd stockpiled, hoping to save them for the move that seemed to be coming faster and faster. Here she was packing for it, and still having no idea where they'd be moving to. Maybe she should look at the condo, even though there'd be no yard. There would, however, be the risk of cranky neighbors. She wondered if dogs were allowed. Because she wanted to get Zach a dog. He deserved it. And after seeing him with Kodi, she knew it would fill an empty space in his heart. One left hollow by his father.

Thinking of Kodi, she couldn't help but think of Ryan. She had to admit, for a brief moment when she was back there, her thoughts had run away on her. He was unlike anyone she'd ever met. Quiet, soulful, yet there were times he seemed to let go. There was something about how those light blue eyes crinkled when he smiled, a rare warmth radiating from him. And there was a tenderness to him that had been surprising. She had seen it that night at the ER when he held and soothed her. Then nearly kissed her.

And yet there was the part of him he kept hidden. The damaged part of him he felt he needed to hide. A part of him that might never open up.

CHAPTER 15

CHRISTMAS EVE MORNING, HOPE WAS up at five. She was running on adrenaline and knew she'd pay the price with a sudden crash, hopefully tomorrow and not during the twelve-hour drive. Tonight was Christmas Eve and she had one thought only: to make this a happy Christmas for Zach. Somehow, she'd make the grueling drive.

She was packing up the trunk when Zach finally came outside with his backpack on. Unlike the last time, he'd listened and put on the jeans and long-sleeved t-shirt she had laid out for him. His jacket was already on the backseat. Unlike their last trip north, as well, he was excited and not sleepy.

She had just shut the backseat door, after making sure he was buckled in and had all of his distractions at hand, especially his electronic games, when she heard Lily call out. She turned to see her running over.

"Lil, you said goodbye last night! You didn't have to get up so early to see us off!"

"No, it's not that, I've got some good news," she said, stopping and catching her breath.

"A new listing?" she asked hopefully.

Lily motioned for her to step away from the car. "Yes! But it's not what you think. Talk about serendipity!"

"Lil, you're making me crazy. What?"

"The deal on this house fell through late last night! I knew you had to get up early so I didn't want to call then."

"Are you serious?"

"Absolutely."

"Can I ... " she couldn't even get the words out. It seemed too good to be true.

"Honey, you can buy it! And not have to move Zach! And still be my next-door neighbor!"

"But didn't those other people pay over his asking price? You know I can't do that."

"Listen, he's already got a contract on another investment property so he wants to get this closed as fast as possible. And it's Christmas so things are dead. You've got an advantage. My lender can get you closed in thirty days."

"Oh, Lil." She glanced over to Zach in the backseat, head down, already playing a game. "This would be the most amazing Christmas present."

"Look, you get going, you've got a crazy long drive ahead of you. I'll call your landlord as soon as it's after nine and tell him you'll pay his asking price and close in thirty days. I think he'll grab it."

She hugged Lily. "Thanks for always looking out for us."

"Hey, we may not have blood, but we're family."

She got in the car and watched Lily walk back to her house. Then she glanced over at the house she and Zach had been living in for the past three years. This could finally give them the roots she'd been longing for. The home and security Zach needed. She could put a basketball hoop in the driveway. Maybe she'd even get a small above-ground pool next summer for those hot summer nights that began in May in the south. And she was definitely getting him a dog.

She pulled away thinking about not just keeping her job but getting the promotion. And now, not having to move and rent again, but possibly owning this very house. It was all amazing. But she said nothing to Zach. Not yet. And she didn't even allow herself to feel excited. That was normal, she told herself. Because what if it didn't work out?

Zach was quiet for the first hour or so of the ride and then he got bored with his video games. She wouldn't let him read, because he tended to get car sick if he did, so they came up with other ways to pass the time. He regaled her with riddles she couldn't seem to ever guess. Then she played "I Spy" which usually involved a nearby car or upcoming sign. After lunch, which was quick, they even sang Christmas carols, which helped to get the excitement going again. And helped give her a second wind. After eating, she'd gotten so tired she almost pulled into a rest stop to close her eyes. Instead, she stopped again and got a sixteen-ounce hot coffee which blessedly did the trick.

As they drew closer, Zach finally fell asleep for a while. During that time, Hope let her mind wander, imagining the coming weeks. Would she really be unpacking the boxes and putting things back into the drawers and closets she'd just taken them out of? She pictured Zach and Jackson playing in an above-ground pool in the yard. She even started thinking she'd have to fence in the yard for Zach's new dog. Was it really all going to happen? It was all so overwhelming, this sudden change in her luck, yet she almost felt numb. But she reminded herself that was to be expected. Especially now, emotionally exhausted and pushing herself mile after mile to get back to Hackettstown and surprise her dad.

They got burgers for supper and ate while she drove. Zach couldn't stop talking about their arrival, which was now just a few hours away. It had been dark for several hours when they crossed into New Jersey and Zach fell asleep again. As they drove past Budd Lake, she glanced back to see him opening his eyes.

"Are we almost there?" he asked.

"We are. We'll be going down the mountain soon."

"I can't wait to surprise Grandpa."

"Me, too."

"You should go to the Jingle Ball, Mom."

"I don't think so. It really has been a long day and I'm exhausted. And tomorrow is Christmas! You're usually up at the crack of dawn," she laughed.

"I could sleep later."

"It's okay, you just get up when you wake up."

"Hey, my ears are popping."

"Yup, we're starting to go down the mountain."

"Are you still sad about the star, Mom?"

"No, I'm fine, Honey. How could I not be, I've got—" Her

215

words caught in her throat as she gasped, her eyes widening, and she pulled over to the side of the road. "Zach! Look!"

She glanced in her rearview mirror and saw Zach's face suddenly light up.

"Mom, it's the star! It's lit!"

"It is! Oh, Zach, I can't believe it!"

They sat there on the side of the road, looking across the valley at the Christmas Star shining high up in the sky over Hackettstown. It was stunning.

"Wow! You were right, Mom. It does look like a giant star in the sky."

"That's because in the dark you can't see Buck Hill."

"So it's all lit up right next to Ryan's house?"

"Yes … it is."

"But how did it happen?"

"I have no idea, Honey. But it's lit! That's all that matters."

"It's so beautiful, Mom."

Tears sprang into her eyes. "Oh, it is, isn't it?"

"It must be really bright on top of the mountain by Ryan's house."

"Yes, it must be."

She pulled back onto the road, wondering how this could have happened. Had he left town? How could he even bear the lights? It didn't seem possible. And it didn't make sense. Not after what she'd learned. She continued down the mountain and eventually onto Main Street.

"Mom, look at all the people!" Zach said, his voice filled with excitement.

There were crowds on the sidewalks and street corners

pointing up to the top of Buck Hill.

"It's just unbelievable," she whispered.

On the far side of town, she turned onto her dad's street and as she got closer, she could see him and Julia in the driveway, looking up at the star. She parked in front of a neighbor's house, so they wouldn't see her car.

"Come on, Zach, let's be quiet so they don't see us right away."

He was out of the car before she was and as they walked down, her son took her hand, pulling her faster. As they got closer, she could see her father was all dressed up in a black suit and his vintage red plaid bow tie she remembered him wearing every Christmas Eve. Julia was beside him in a gorgeous green taffeta gown.

When they were almost to the driveway, Zach broke loose and began to run.

"Grandpa!"

Her father turned and his eyes widened in shock. And then his face crumpled with emotion as he ran to Zach, pulling him into a bear hug. Tears were already streaming down her own cheeks.

"Oh, Hope!" Julia called out and ran to give her a hug.

"We're here for Christmas!" Zach shouted as her father finally let him go. "And the star is shining!"

Now they were all laughing and giddy with joy. Her father looked at her with such tenderness. "I'm so happy you came back, Hope."

She walked right into his arms.

"Thank you," he whispered into her ear. "This is the best

Christmas present I could have ever asked for."

"Me, too, Dad." Then she pulled away and looked at him. "Dad, how did this happen? The star being lit?"

He shook his head. "I really can't say, Honey."

"But Ryan? He let this happen?"

He shrugged. "It sure looks that way."

They all stood there looking at the star. It was such a magical sight it was hard to turn away.

"I can't believe it," she said as she stared at it. "But there's something ... different looking about it, don't you think?"

"It actually looks more like the star did when I was a boy and we put it up and took it down each year. A bit more ... rustic, I guess you'd say."

"Yes, you're right."

"It's just so wonderful," Julia chimed in. "Especially that you're both here to see it."

"Mom, are you so happy now?" Zach asked.

She looked at her son who was grinning from ear to ear, and then her dad, his eyes still shining with emotion.

"I couldn't be happier, Zach."

"Mom!" he said then, as something occurred to him. "Tonight I can make my first wish on the star!"

She nodded then, suddenly so filled with emotion herself she couldn't trust herself to speak. Her father ruffled Zach's hair.

"But first, we're all going to the Jingle Ball," Julia said, taking her dad's arm.

"Oh, no, we can't possibly. We've had a long day and Zach is so—"

218

"I'm not tired!" Zach insisted before she could finish. "Are you tired, Mom?"

And suddenly, she had to admit it. Her earlier exhaustion was gone. Excitement seemed to course through her veins. "Oh, but we didn't bring anything to wear. Just jeans and sweaters," she said.

"Not to worry. I think I've got something that will do just fine," her father said with a secretive smile.

She had a feeling she knew what he meant. "But Dad, I packed all Mom's things away and donated them."

Her father shook his head insistently. "Not this, Honey."

She looked at Zach. "Okay, then, it looks like we're all going to the Jingle Ball!"

CHAPTER 16

SHE QUICKLY GOT ZACH DRESSED. Then she couldn't help it, she laid on her bed with her head on her pillow and looked out the window. And there it was, as it had always been, the star shining on Buck Hill. As it had done for all of the Christmases of her youth. In the years that she hadn't come home after marrying Drew—and there were too many of them—she imagined it. Longed for it. Feeling deep in her soul that to be able to wish on it once again could somehow make her prayers come true. Because, though it was just a man-made star, to her it was tied to something divine.

"It's back, Mom," she whispered in the dark room.

She felt a wish, a prayer, somewhere deep in her chest, but she couldn't seem to pull it out. It was a longing. But hadn't all of her wishes come true already? Of course, they had.

Finally, she got up and began to dress.

Ten minutes later, Hope walked down the stairs to find them waiting for her. She was wearing her mother's white velvet gown, the one she'd worn every Christmas that Hope could remember. When she first slipped it on, she could almost hear her mother's voice in her bedroom, as she had all those years ago when her mother would come in wearing it to help Hope get dressed. *This is my favorite night of the year,* she would say. And Hope would always reply, *Mommy you look so beautiful.*

Now it was Zach, looking up at her who said, "Mom, you look so beautiful."

She knelt down to hug him and repeated her own mother's words, "This is my favorite night of the year."

He was wearing the white button-down shirt and cardigan she'd brought for Christmas dinner. And with it, her father's plaid bow tie that he wore each year that matched her mother's dress.

"Oh, Hope. Zach is right, you look stunning. That was your mother's favorite gown."

"That you do," her dad said, his eyes misty, "and I have something that will go with it perfectly."

He turned and opened the closet door and took out a red velvet cape with a white fur muff to match the dress.

"Oh! Oh, Dad! I thought that was long gone!"

Her father shook his head and she could see he was too emotional to speak. He draped the cape around her shoulders and then kissed her cheek. "I kept it in our bedroom closet all this time. Now, turn around."

She turned slowly as they all watched her.

"You're as beautiful as your mother," he said.

"It's just perfect, Hope," Julia said, squeezing her hand.

"Mom, you look like a princess."

"And you, young man, look very grown up."

"This is Grandpa's favorite tie."

"I know. My mom picked it out to match this dress and cape."

She picked up the fur muff, threw in her cell and tissues, which she had a feeling she'd need, into the little zipper compartment, then held out her arm and hooked it through Zach's. "I couldn't imagine a more handsome escort."

Her father took Julia's arm then, clearing his throat. Hope knew how moving this night must be for him. As it was for her. Clearing her throat, she said, "Now, let's go have some fun."

And they walked out the door.

Parking would be tough, so they decided to walk. It was a mild winter evening and there was little wind, so even in their evening clothes, they weren't really cold. As they reached Main Street, they could hear the music from several blocks away. Groups of people were still stopping here and there, looking up at the star in awe, gone for so many years and now magically appearing again. They passed the gazebo, which resembled a giant ornament, draped in glittering garland and ablaze with twinkling white lights. The town Christmas tree was radiant, its snow-covered branches glowing in different colors from the big old-fashioned lights.

As they crossed Moore Street, they saw the big white tent erected in the parking lot behind Stella's Café. Just then tiny snowflakes began to fall from the sky.

The night couldn't have been more perfect, Hope thought. But there was one thing still needed. An answer to how the star came to be lit. And there seemed to be only one person who could give her the answer, Ryan. Was he even still in town? Even if he was, she doubted he would be coming to the Jingle Ball.

The four of them walked into the white tent and Zach gasped. Soft white lights were strung across the top of the tent with sparkling snowflakes dangling from the center and all along the sides. Small Christmas trees were in the corners, also lit up with white lights. Tables were scattered along the perimeter of the tent with red tablecloths and candles flickering on each. The band was playing "Rockin' Around the Christmas Tree," and people were dancing. Her eyes scanned the crowd looking for Ryan, who was, of course, nowhere to be seen.

"Hope, you did it!"

She turned to see Phoebe running toward her, dressed in a midnight blue skirt and white lace top, blinking red Christmas ornaments hanging from her ears. And then she noticed her dad and Julia giving each other a strange look. Before she even could ask what that was about, her dad started leading Zach away.

"I bet Zach is ready for Christmas cookies," he suggested.

"And hot cocoa!" Zach agreed enthusiastically.

"Hope, why don't you mingle," Julia added. "We'll be with Zach over by the refreshments."

Phoebe took her arm before she could even respond to Julia.

"How did you do it! Tell me!" Phoebe insisted.

"Pheebs, I had nothing to do with the star getting lit tonight. I have no idea how it happened. But honestly, something doesn't make sense here. I mean, there wasn't enough money in the fund, right?"

"Right, but whatever happened, I'm glad it did. Everyone is! And Hope, you certainly were part of making it happen, whether you want to admit it or not. You were the one who got people excited again with your article. And believing again. You started it all."

"I guess … " At that moment she saw Ryan walk into the tent. He was wearing a dark suit and tie and looked so handsome he nearly took her breath away. And then he saw her and stopped. Her heart began to race. For a long moment, they just stared at each other.

"Pheebs, if you'll excuse me, I see someone who must know the answer to our mystery."

Phoebe turned to see where she was looking. "Good luck," she whispered.

As she began walking toward him, Hope saw Lauren emerge from the crowd and take his arm, pulling Ryan onto the dance floor. A moment later they disappeared amongst the dancing couples. Just then someone tapped her on the shoulder and she turned to see Mr. Durling, who held out his hand. She took it and followed him onto the dance floor.

"I am so glad to see you, Mr. Durling. Can you please tell me how on earth the star is up and lit?"

"Hope, I was just about to ask you the same thing. When I walked outside tonight and saw it … I was stunned!"

"So, the crew we put together didn't have anything to do with this?"

"No, they didn't. In fact, I haven't talked to one person who knows anything about it."

"I don't get it."

She kept catching glimpses of Ryan dancing with Lauren through the crowd. Lauren was smiling ear to ear, gazing up at him adoringly. Ironically, the band was playing a slow version of "All I Want for Christmas is You." And it was obvious, that was how Lauren felt about him. Whatever she said next had him laughing and Hope felt her stomach twist into a knot.

"Well thank you for the dance," Mr. Durling said, and she realized the song was over.

She made her way through the crowd on the dance floor to look for Ryan again as the crowd began to move about. She zig-zagged around, then spotted him near the refreshment table talking to Zach. Zach looked so happy. She paused, watching as Ryan showed Zach something on his cell phone and Zach began to nod. Suddenly, as if sensing her watching, Ryan looked up at her. He said something to Zach and then came toward her.

"You look beautiful, Hope."

"Thank you, Ryan. You look pretty nice yourself."

"I can't remember the last time I wore a suit," he laughed.

"I'm actually kind of surprised to see you here."

He didn't answer. Instead, he held out a hand as the band began to play "Have Yourself A Merry Little Christmas."

"Would you like to dance?"

"Yes," she said, stepping closer.

His arm wound around her back, pulling her close to him, and she put a hand on his shoulder, her other hand held firmly in his as they began to move slowly across the dance floor. He was staring into her eyes and she couldn't seem to speak.

"Will you tell me how this happened?" she managed finally.

"What are you talking about?" he answered with a tiny smile.

"Come on, Ryan. The star lighting up tonight? It seems to be a big mystery. I've asked pretty much everyone in town and no one knows how it happened."

He shrugged.

"They're calling it a miracle."

"I wouldn't go that far."

She stopped dancing and they stood there. "Ryan, please be honest with me."

The little smile grew. "Let's just say ... I saw the light."

"Haha. Good pun. But I'm serious. That doesn't answer my questions."

He looked away a moment and sighed as if he really didn't want to get into it. Then he turned to her again. "I like this town, Hope. And I like the people. They've been nothing but kind and welcoming to me. And to be completely honest, when I thought about leaving here, I realized I didn't want to."

"I'm glad to hear that."

He looked at her a long moment. "Sometimes it's easier to run away from things than to face them head-on. I realized after you left that I've been doing that my whole life. And people have always left me so ... why not just leave them first. It's what I've always done."

"Oh, Ryan."

"I've never really belonged anywhere before, except the service. Home wasn't ever something I thought about. But since

I've come here to this little town, I see now why people want
it. And don't want to lose it. That saying that you told me of
your mother's, *When you see the star, you'll know——*"

His voice was suddenly drowned out by a loud drum roll.
The band leader took the mic, asking for everyone's attention.
A moment later, Lauren stepped onto the stage with a big smile.
Hope tried not to roll her eyes.

"Merry Christmas, everyone! The Chamber of Commerce
would like to thank you all for attending tonight's Jingle Ball
and for participating in all of the Hometown Holiday events.
I'd say this might be the best one yet."

The crowd broke into applause and nodded in agreement.
She glanced at Ryan, who watched Lauren, his face unreadable.

"I would like to say a special thank you," Lauren went on
after the applause died down, "to our own Ryan Miller, who
restored all of the vintage ornaments to replace those damaged
in the superstorm, but also because he … donated his entire
payment right back into next year's Hometown Holiday fund!"

Everyone began clapping and turning, looking for Ryan,
who was blushing and horrified at the attention.

"To Ryan!" Lauren toasted, raising her glass as the crowd
followed suit.

Then Lauren looked right at him and blew him a kiss.
Hope nearly felt her jaw drop. What a fool she'd been. She
turned to him, but people were coming over and grabbing his
hand to shake. She began walking away.

"Hope, don't——"

She turned to see him following her.

"Wait," he said.

She stopped. Just then her phone rang inside the muff. She turned to him. "I'm sorry, I've been waiting for an important call," she said, glad for the excuse. She headed to a quiet corner of the tent, not realizing he was still following her.

"Lily, hi," she said.

She listened as Lily explained what happened with her offer.

"Really? Oh … that is so great."

"Why doesn't your voice sound like it's so great," Lily asked.

"I'm just someplace where it's loud, that's all. Yes, email it to me and I'll sign and get it right back to you. And yes, it's a wonderful Christmas gift. Thank you."

She hung up, a bit dazed, and turned to see Ryan close enough to hear everything.

"Sounds like you just got some good news."

"I … did, yes. I just bought a house. The one Zach and I have been renting."

He looked stunned. "And this is what you really want?"

"It's what Zach needs. We won't have to move. His friends, his school, none of that will have to change now. Our lives are down there. It seems everything we wished for, including the Christmas Star, is coming true."

He looked at her as if searching for something. And then, in a cold voice said, "That's great, Hope. I'm sure you'll both be very happy."

"I hope you and Lauren are, too," she said, in an equally cold voice.

Just then Zach appeared with her dad and Julia, all of them smiling, unaware of what had just happened.

"I think a certain young man would like to dance with his mother," her father announced as the band began "I'll Be Home for Christmas."

Ryan nodded and walked away without a word.

"What's wrong with Ryan?" her dad asked.

"Remember? Christmas isn't his thing?"

Then she gave her attention to her son, who held her hand and put an arm around her back. He was smiling up at her as he swayed side to side, barely moving at all, and she followed suit. Over his head, she could see Ryan exiting the tent where Lauren was standing. She turned and followed him.

In that moment, any little moments of doubt she may have had about her future were laid to rest. She was buying a house, Zach was staying put, everything was working out. She was a fool to open her heart to the possibility of something with Ryan. She'd been telling herself it was impossible all along. And now ... wasn't fate showing her the way? And wasn't it all working out like its own little miracle?

CHAPTER 17

HOPE SAT ON THE BACK deck on a rocking chair in the dark, still wearing her cape, a fleece blanket also wrapped around her. Looking up at the star, she still couldn't quite believe it. Here she was, in her mother's gown and cape, a mother herself now, and having just tucked her little boy into bed as he gazed out the window at this very star.

Zach hadn't said much as he lay down, exhausted from the long day's drive and then the Jingle Ball. He laid on the pillow and turned to look out as she watched him, her heart overflowing with emotion. He needed a haircut, she'd realized, but it had been overlooked in the craziness of the past weeks. She was starting to see little changes in his features, a glimmer of the young man he would soon become.

"I'm glad we came back, Mom," he said, turning to look at her.

"Me, too, because we would have missed the star."

"I'm not upset about Hawaii anymore, so don't be sad, okay?"

"Oh, Zach … "

"Grandpa was so happy."

"I know. And Zach, I'm not sad. How can I be? Everything is working out so beautifully. I didn't tell you yet, but we don't have to move, after all. I'm buying our house and we'll be staying put, right next door to Lily. You can stay in your same school and little league. And Jackson can come anytime."

His eyes widened.

"And ... I think maybe we'll get a pool this summer."

"Wow, Mom," he said, not as enthusiastic as she thought he'd be. But then he yawned, long and loud and she laughed. Of course, he was too tired to react. Tomorrow it would hit him and he'd probably be bouncing off the walls.

"Okay, Honey, we can talk about all of that tomorrow. After we open presents!" She ruffled his hair. "Now, you need to get right to sleep."

She'd kissed his cheek and he immediately turned over.

Now she sat there rocking, so grateful that fate had somehow brought them back so that Zach could see the star. Because soon it would all change for good. Her father would be moving to Florida. They would close on their house. And life, she knew, would probably never bring another opportunity for him to see it. Her heart felt so heavy at the realization.

She turned as the back door opened to see her father coming outside in his winter parka with two steaming mugs in his hands. He gave her one and then sat beside her in the other rocking chair. They both looked up at the star silently for a long moment.

"You okay, Honey?" he asked after a while.

"I am, Dad. I'm just sitting here thinking about how ...

things have worked out." She turned to him then. "I didn't have a chance to tell you, but I'm buying the house I've been renting, so Zach and I won't have to move. He'll keep his school, his friends ... everything I was hoping for worked out."

"That's wonderful, Hope. But ... you don't seem happy. What is it?"

She sat there, unable to speak. Looking up at the star again, she felt almost ungrateful.

"I'm so blessed, aren't I? I've got my job, with a promotion and a raise. I'm getting the house. It's what Zach wants, not to move again or change schools. It's just ... " She turned to her father, her throat clogging with tears. "I'm not really sure it's what I still want. And I feel so guilty about that."

Her dad leaned over and took both her hands. "Honey, did it ever occur to you that Zach wanted that because he thinks it would make you happy?"

"What? What do you mean?"

"Zach worries about you. He's ... well, he's an old soul, just like your mother always called you. Zach knows that's what you want."

"But he has his school and friends, his soccer team. He's finally settled. You know we bounced around so much and it wasn't always easy for him. You're right, he's a really sensitive kid and he wasn't always accepted right away in the different schools and that was hard on him."

"Hope, Zach has made a few friends here, too. Julia's grandson, for one. And you know first-hand that our schools are top-notch. Plus ... there's a perfectly good home right here," he said, nodding to the house behind them."

MARYANN MCFADDEN

She stared at him, her eyes widening. "Dad, what are you saying?"

Suddenly, he couldn't look at her. His face flushed, and he seemed almost shy. Then he glanced up at the star before looking back at her. "Hope, I've asked Julia to marry me. I hope you approve."

Her mouth dropped open. "What!" She jumped up and hugged him. "Oh, Dad, of course I do. I know Mom would approve, too."

For a long moment, she could see her dad struggling for words, his face full of emotion. She sat back in her rocker, giving him time. He'd never been one for displays of emotion, she'd known that all of her life.

"We're … " He cleared his throat and began again, "We're not moving away."

"You're not going to Florida?"

He shook his head. "I realized this is always going to be home. I don't want to leave Hackettstown, and neither does Julia. We've both been here all of our lives. Our friends, our memories … it's all here. So, we're going to live in Julia's house next door. It's small and all on one floor, so better suited to us old folks," he finished with a chuckle.

"Oh, Dad, that's wonderful."

He grew serious again. "Hope, this house is yours, for you and Zach. If you want it."

The emotion she herself had been fighting all night suddenly spilled over and a sob escaped her. She couldn't believe this.

"Oh, Dad," she finally managed, "I don't know what to say."

233

"You don't have to say anything. I know it's a lot to process, so just think about it. And whatever you decide, it's fine. There's no wrong decision here. I just want you to know you have a choice."

"Thank you."

"Now, it's late and I think we should both get some sleep. Tomorrow's Christmas!"

"Yes, it is."

She leaned over and kissed his cheek. Then they both stood up to go inside.

"Hopefully Zach is finally asleep. He was beyond tired, but every time I went upstairs, he was still lying there and looking out the window at the star."

"Just like a little girl I once knew."

She smiled, then opened the back door. Her dad hesitated.

"Aren't you coming?"

"I think I'll just stay out here a little longer."

When she was gone, Red McClain looked up at the Christmas Star he'd known his entire seventy-two years and smiled through his tears. "We raised a good one, Alice," he whispered.

It was after eleven when Hope went upstairs to finally go to sleep. Though she was exhausted, her mind raced. How could it not? Everything had changed tonight in so many ways she couldn't have predicted. Hopefully, after a good night's sleep, things would be much clearer in the morning. But right now, it was as if her heart was torn in two.

As she tiptoed down the hall and got closer to the bedroom, she could hear a voice. It was Zach! But who would he be talking to? She slipped off her shoes and went as quietly as she could to the door, which was slightly ajar. Peeking in, she saw her son, wide awake and standing at the window looking up.

"I have one more wish and this one is the biggest," she heard her son say. "I wish I could tell my mom how Ryan got the star fixed but it has to be a secret. I think he likes my mom and I think she likes him, too. Maybe if she knew she'd want to stay here."

Her hand went to her chest and once again her eyes filled. How could there possibly be any more surprises on this night? Turning, she quietly slipped downstairs and went to get her coat from the closet. Just then her father came into the foyer.

"Where on earth are you going at this hour?" he asked.

"Dad, I need to talk to Ryan."

"Now?"

"Yes, now."

And she rushed out the front door.

It began to snow again as she backed out of the driveway and headed toward Buck Hill. It was a gentle snow still, as earlier, with no wind, and she could see just fine, thank goodness. She made her way slowly up the dirt driveway, the light of the star guiding her. She'd never seen it up close, not in all her years in town. She couldn't believe it was even happening.

When she got to the top of the hill it was bright as day and she sat there a moment, her car all lit up inside as if it was sitting under a spotlight. She turned off the car and got out. And then she slowly looked up, the sudden intense light causing her to squint. The star rose up to the heavens, its brightness lighting up the trees surrounding the clearing like sentinels at attention, guarding its presence. She stood there in awe, a catch in her throat at its magnificence up close.

Just then she heard the workshop door open and Kodi bark. She turned to see Ryan coming out, still dressed in his suit and tie. Oddly, he was wearing sunglasses. Kodi ran up to her and sat, whining to be petted. She stroked his head as Ryan came closer, then stopped suddenly. Even in his sunglasses, without being able to read his eyes, she could tell he was stunned.

"Hope, what are you doing here?"

"I need to know something, Ryan," she said, her voice trembling with nervousness. "How did you do this?"

He stood there a long moment, then shrugged, looking away. Then he turned back to her for a second before walking back to the workshop door, opening it, and she thought he was going to shut it and shut her out. But he motioned for her to follow him in. When she stepped inside, he shut the door behind her, took off the sunglasses and blinked a few moments as his eyes adjusted.

"How?" she repeated. "Please tell me."

"I didn't do anything."

"Stop it, Ryan. I know. I heard Zach making a wish on that star," she said, gesturing outside. "Wishing that I would find out it was all you."

She realized something suddenly and turned, opening the door and peeking outside before closing it again. "Where's all the lumber for your workshop expansion?"

He sighed, shaking his head as if giving up. "Well don't look too close at your star because it's not pretty. It's kind of jerry-rigged for now because I had to add wood to the metal. It's a temporary fix, just to get it lit for Christmas Eve."

"But, Ryan, the light from it. How are you able—"

He put a hand up, stopping her words. "It's fine."

She stood there, shaking her head. Frustrated and yet so moved by his selflessness. "Ryan, come on. Don't be mad, but my dad, who thinks the world of you by the way, told me."

Ryan sighed, shaking his head, obviously not happy.

"Please," she said softly.

He rubbed his face with his hands, then he began to pace for a few minutes, and she could see him thinking. Finally, he turned and looked right at her and began to talk.

"I've had issues with bright lights since … Iraq and what happened that day. Sometimes it can trigger a flashback of that moment … the explosion. And it's like I'm there again, and it's actually happening, the noise, the screaming, the blinding flash. I couldn't even see for a few days afterwards but that healed. Kind of like snow blindness they explained. The flashbacks, though, they never really went away. I should have dealt with it long ago. I was supposed to but … sometimes it's easier to avoid what we don't want to face. So, I kind of learned how to do that."

"Like I did with my father."

He nodded. "But you finally faced your father and made things right. And I … I finally went back to the VA. Turns out that avoiding triggers is pretty common and I don't want to do that anymore. I don't want it controlling my life anymore. So ... I'm doing something called exposure therapy."

"That's wonderful, Ryan."

"That star ... it's kind of like homework for me. It'll take some time but ... " he picked up the sunglasses with a little smile, "I'll wear these for a while."

"But why would you do all this? You didn't have to light the star. You had no legal obligation."

"I know that. But a certain young boy told me that first morning he came up here that he thought the star would make his mom happy again. That she'd been sad for a long time."

"Oh my ... Zach told you that?"

Ryan nodded.

She stood there, stunned. "What else did he tell you?"

He hesitated.

"Ryan, please."

"He knows you really want to live back south but ... he'd like to live here, near his grandfather."

Her throat ached with the tears she was trying so desperately to hold back. How was it possible she'd missed all this. "So, he wished for me to keep my job, the house, all of it ... to make *me* happy? My dad was right. He is an old soul."

"He's quite a kid, Hope."

"And you, Ryan ... you're quite a guy doing all of this, putting yourself through this, for my son."

But Ryan was shaking his head. "I did it for you, Hope."

She stared at him as his words sank in.

"I've never seen someone with so much determination. And love. And to me ... that's not something I ever got to

238

experience. That to me is a miracle. And I … I wanted you to have one of your own."

"Oh, Ryan, I … I don't know what to say."

He came closer, his voice almost a whisper now. "Hope, I would do anything for you. Don't you know that by now?"

"But what about Lauren?"

"There's never been anything between us. Not that she hasn't tried."

"But how did you even know we were coming back here? Because I wasn't planning to come back for Christmas."

"I didn't. I was going to leave the star lit until you eventually did come back. However many weeks or months that might have taken. Even if it took all year until next Christmas."

As her father did for her mother all those decades ago. Tears spilled down her cheeks.

"I do believe in miracles, Hope," he said, coming closer and closer as he spoke. "The fact that I survived that explosion in Iraq and I'm here, that's one. Meeting you … that's another. Then you coming back unexpectedly like this on Christmas Eve … yet another."

He was just a few inches away now and slowly he lowered his head until his mouth touched hers. His kiss was soft and gentle and as she wrapped her arms around his neck, he pulled her into him, holding her so close she could feel his heart beating as their kisses deepened.

He pulled back then and cupped her face in his hands. "Don't leave, Hope. Stay here."

"Oh, Ryan, I'm not leaving. This … this is home."

He put his sunglasses on then and led her outside again.

They stood under the star and he held her as she looked up, thinking about the miracle that was happening in that very moment.

CHAPTER 18

HOPE WASN'T SURE EXACTLY WHEN she finally fell asleep. She'd stayed at Ryan's for a long time, talking, kissing, hardly able to believe it was real. When she got into bed and began to doze, what had just happened would hit her all over again and her eyes would fly open to make sure she wasn't dreaming. In the dark, with Zach breathing softly in the bed beside her, she kept reliving Ryan looking at her with such desire in the moment before he kissed her that she felt she might be melting inside. She smiled in the dark then, giddy with excitement. How could she possibly sleep?

The next thing she knew, it seemed as if it was five minutes later and Zach was jumping on her bed.

"Mom, it's Christmas! Wake up!"

"Oh, Zach, it's so early," she said, barely able to open her eyes.

"Mom, it's already light out. I slept late for Christmas!"

And then she remembered the night before. Ryan. She pulled Zach down into her arms.

"Merry Christmas, my snuggle bunny!"

"Mom!" he admonished her on the babyish name this time. "Come on, I think Grandpa's already up!"

She pulled on her robe and they went downstairs. She was surprised to see her dad and Julia were already seated in the family room with coffee. The tree was lit and surrounded with presents. Zach ran right up to her dad and gave him a hug.

"Merry Christmas, Zach. I think Santa brought you a whole bunch of presents under our tree."

Zach gave her dad a look. She wasn't sure if he did or didn't believe anymore, but neither of them said a word about it.

"Merry Christmas, Hope," Julia said and got up and gave her a hug.

"Merry Christmas, Julia," she said, then whispered, "I'm so happy for you and my dad."

"Thank you, dear."

Zach sat under the tree. "I'm ready!"

Hope went and sat on the floor beside him and began handing Zach his gifts. They all watched with delight as he opened each one. He was on his third when there was a loud knock on the front door.

"Who on earth could that be on Christmas morning?" her dad said.

"Zach, would you see who that is please?" she asked quickly, giving her dad a wink and a nod to stay seated.

Zach ran out into the foyer and threw the door open and Hope watched as his face lit up to find Ryan and Kodi standing there.

"Ryan!"

"Merry Christmas, Buddy," Ryan said, smiling and giving Zach a hug.

"Mom, it's Ryan," he shouted, turning and realizing then that she was right behind him.

"Yes, I see. I actually invited Ryan to share our Christmas."

"Cool! Ryan, I have a present for you."

They went back into the family room. Zach ran and grabbed a small wrapped package and handed it to Ryan. Kodi was following Zach's every move. Ryan untied the string and tore the paper off, holding up a star ornament made of Popsicle sticks and glitter.

"Grandpa helped me make it before we left so you wouldn't forget me. And now you can ... oops." He gave Ryan a look of alarm.

"It's okay, Zach. I know it was Ryan who fixed the star. I kind of figured it out and then Ryan told me the rest."

He looked at Ryan. "You're not mad?"

"Of course not. In fact, I think your mom might have a little secret she wants to tell you."

He turned to look at her.

"Zach, would you like to stay here in Hackettstown? Live in this very house?"

He looked at her in shock. "For real?"

"Is that okay, Honey?" she asked, suddenly worried.

He broke into the biggest smile she'd ever seen.

"Really, Mom? With Grandpa?"

"Well, Grandpa is actually going to live next door with Julia. They're getting married."

Zach looked at Red and Julia in awe. Then he looked at

Ryan, and finally her.

"Mom, this is all the things I wished for on the star. I mean at first I didn't but then … I hope that's okay."

"I know, Zach. And it's all okay because somehow with the star things usually turn out the way they're meant to."

"But what about your new job?" he asked, suddenly concerned.

"I have a standing offer at the *Gazette* here in town. It's where I originally started working as a writer."

"Mom, this is the best Christmas ever!"

Zach came and gave her the tightest hug, holding onto her for such a long time.

"Honey, I think you've got a few more to unwrap under there," she said, "but how about first we give Grandpa and Julia their presents?"

Zach went to the back of the tree and picked up two more gifts, went over to his grandfather and Julia, and handed them both their presents. Julia unwrapped a small box and pulled out a gold charm bracelet, gasping.

"This was your mother's!"

"Yes, it was. Zach and I wanted to thank you for all of your help. When we went through her jewelry box, he thought you'd like this out of everything else after I explained that you probably took part in so many of what those charms represented."

"Oh, Hope, Zach, thank you." Julia held out her arm and Red put the bracelet on her wrist. "I'll treasure it."

Then her dad tore open his box, lifted the lid, and laughed as he held up a brightly printed shirt covered in palm trees.

"We thought you might wear that in Florida, but … how

about I exchange it for another flannel shirt instead?" Hope said, laughing along with everyone else.

"You know what? I think I'll keep it. I'll be quite fashionable at barbeques next summer," he said with a chuckle.

"Is it my turn, again?" Zach asked, practically bouncing up and down now.

"Absolutely," Hope said.

Zach went back by the tree and began sorting through presents again, with Kodi sitting right by his side. Hope glanced over at Ryan, who was standing on the other side of the tree. She walked over to him and he put an arm around her as they watched Zach opening more gifts.

"Who's ready for coffee and scones?" Julia asked, standing up and heading into the kitchen.

Everyone said yes.

As Zach continued opening and Julia began bringing cups and plates into the room, Ryan pulled her behind the Christmas tree.

"Still not really into Christmas?" she teased.

He laughed. "I think Zach is right. This is the best Christmas ever."

Then he pulled her close, wrapping his arms around her and kissing her lips, then her neck, and she breathed him in, so happy she thought her heart might burst.

"Merry Christmas, Hope. I hope this is the first of many for us," he whispered in her ear.

"Merry Christmas, Ryan. I have no doubt it is."

When the presents were over, her dad and Julia left to visit her family. They were holding hands and she felt both happy and wistful watching them. There would never be another Christmas with her mother. But in that moment, she felt her mother's presence as surely as if she were there. She walked over to the big picture window overlooking the yard and looked up. The star was still shining, as it would all Christmas Day. She whispered aloud her mother's words, as she would every December from now on.

When you see the star, you'll know you're home.

The End

ACKNOWLEDGEMENTS

EVERY BOOK IS SPECIAL TO an author, but this one is particularly dear to me. I first saw the Christmas Star when my family moved to Hackettstown in 1964 from Brooklyn. For this little girl, it seemed magical as it shined each December on a mountain across the valley of our little town. Now, many years later, it still holds a special place in my heart because, like Hope, I can see it from my bedroom window. It has become a tradition for my grandchildren to come for sleepovers to see the star.

It was my mother, during a Hallmark Christmas movie, who said, "You should write about the star." She loved those movies! I began a screenplay, but another book pushed that aside until Covid hit. I couldn't seem to write anything in those first months. While walking through my neighborhood one evening during the first days of lockdown, I looked up to see the star shining as night fell. It was April! Tears filled my eyes and hope filled my heart. I went home and in the following months, finished the screenplay. Then wrote the novel.

I have so many to thank in the journey of writing this story. If I've forgotten someone, I beg your forgiveness.

Thanks to Dale Durling, for sharing his knowledge of star history, structure, and electrical information; Paul Stahl for sharing his knowledge of star history; our own Hometown Holiday crew and many volunteers who make Christmas in Hackettstown truly like a Hallmark movie.

For reading early versions: Robin Hoffman Abourizk, Debora Messina, Loretta Mizeski, Sue Gardener, and Janet Bejarano. Michael Mizeski, who cheered me on since reading the screenplay and added some male perspective. And Kathy Ulisse for a very detailed proofread. Any errors are mine alone!

For Colleen Bain at Centenary University Library and all of the booksellers and librarians for their cherished support.

My sister, Jacky Abromitis, for all tech and web support. She is amazing!

My dear writing partner, Julie Maloney, who is my first reader, biggest supporter, and someone who makes this crazy writing life bearable at times. I love US. I can't imagine doing this without you.

And to my kids, Patrick and Marisa, whose love and belief in me inspire me and keep me happy even on the toughest days. They are both incredible writers!

I wish the late Frank Miller, my brother's father-in-law, was here to see this book. He was such a wonderful help in the writing of the script that was the genesis of this novel.

This book is also for the people of Hackettstown. Those who erected that first star to welcome our soldiers home from World War II. The late Dr. Stanowicz and his family, who kept the star lit for many, many years after building their house on Buck Hill. And now the Huff family, who is keeping the tradition alive each Christmas, as well as lighting the cross each Easter. We appreciate you more than you can know.

And to all who will be looking up at the star this holiday season, sharing your own stories and making your own memories of our Christmas Star, thank you.

PLEASE BE CONSIDERATE OF OUR STAR

WHILE THE CHRISTMAS STAR IS real, it is meant to be viewed and enjoyed from a distance. It is on private property and no trespassing is allowed. Please honor the family that keeps the star lit by respecting their privacy.

Trespassers will be subject to arrest and prosecution.